Who is Annabell?

A Short Fantasy Story
Young Adults

Written by
Alan Davies

MAPLE
PUBLISHERS

Who is Annabell? - A Short Fantasy Story Young Adults

Author: Alan Davies

Copyright © 2025 Alan Davies

The right of Alan Davies to be identified as author of this work has been asserted by the author in accordance with section 77 and 78 of the Copyright, Designs and Patents Act 1988.

First Published in 2024

ISBN 978-1-83538-536-4 (Paperback)
    978-1-83538-552-4 (Hardback)
    978-1-83538-537-1 (E-Book)

Book Cover designed by Alan Davies and Book layout by:
    White Magic Studios
    www.whitemagicstudios.co.uk

Published by:
    Maple Publishers
    Fairbourne Drive, Atterbury,
    Milton Keynes,
    MK10 9RG, UK
    www.maplepublishers.com

This book is dedicated to our beautiful angel Serena

Contents

Chapter One
The Find

The catalyst for Annabell's story began in a field somewhere in the Western United States of America in the year 2209 AD

A farmer, Bill Jacobs was ploughing a field. There was nothing particularly special about Bill, he was just an ordinary man of average height, about five foot ten inches tall. He was a bit overweight. His hair was thinning and was now mostly grey with just a few remnants of blond hair which act as a reminder of the once thick curly blond hair of his youth.

Bill has grown a thick beard to offset the lack of hair to his head, his beard was a mixture of grey, blond and ginger.

Bill is now thirty-eight years old. The years of toiling on the land and being out in all weather has taken its toll on his features. His face shows the ravages of his occupation and time. Bill is a happy, jolly man though, and at this moment in time is at peace with himself and the world but this hasn't always been the case.

Nine years previously something happened to Bill that was to change his life drastically.

Bill didn't know it but *today* was the reason why he'd been chosen for something very special to happen.

He's in the field ploughing away, singing as he's ploughing with not a care in the world.

His old tractor which he calls Remi is chugging up and down the field breaking up the hard soil in readiness for its next crop. Sometimes a puff of black/white smoke wafts out of Remi's exhaust as it struggles to pull the heavy plough.

Bill has been ploughing the field for several hours, his large stomach is letting him know that it's ready for something to eat. He pulled up the plough, turned the steering wheel of the tractor and headed for one of his favourite spots to have his lunch. It was an old tree that was situated at the far end of the field that he was ploughing.

Bill drove the tractor towards the tree. As it neared it, several pigeons were spooked and flew off the tree in a great hurry, shedding some of their feathers which fluttered to the ground.

Two crows that were perched at the top of the tree didn't move.

Bill turned off the engine, the tractor spluttered and juddered forward slightly, as if to say it too was grateful for the rest.

Bill got his lunchbox off the tractor and walked under the canopy of the tree. It was noticeably cooler here that's why Bill liked it.

It was a very hot day, this was the perfect spot for him to get out of the sun.

He sat down with his back supported by the tree's trunk. Bill opened his lunchbox and was looking forward to eating its contents. Inside the box were two doorstep size cheese and pickle sandwiches, and a small bowl of salad with a lid on it to keep out the flies.

Bill ate his lunch and put the box on the ground next to him. He then drank a fruit juice to wash down his food.

Bill was feeling tired now, he rested his head on the trunk of the tree and fell asleep. He was woken up by the two crows who were making a racket. Bill wondered what was wrong with the crows. He got up from the ground, stretched his aching back and looked up at the crows and told them to *shush.*

They seemed to be pointing their beaks at him. They were flapping their wings in a frenzy of excitement - it was like they were trying to tell him something. Then all of a sudden the two crows flew down and landed on his lunchbox. Bill thought that they were looking for scraps of food but something strange happened. The crows tried to fly off with the lunchbox but it was too heavy for them.

Bill bent down and picked up the box, as he did this the crows flew away.

Bill looked down to where his lunchbox had been and noticed an object embedded in the soil. He was certain that it hadn't been there when he put the lunchbox down.

He prised the object out of the ground, as it came out he could hear a hissing noise, like gasses being released. Bill had the object in his hand. He looked at it, and looked at it. He was puzzled by the shape of it. It appeared to be one quarter of a circle, it had a hole in its narrowest end. It wasn't very big, only two inches long, and he couldn't feel any weight to it, it was as light as a feather.

There were millions of stones in that field, but this object was something very odd. It wasn't a stone. It was something metallic but not like any metal that he'd ever seen.

Bill looked around the ground to see if he could find anymore pieces of the object but there weren't any.

He put it into his pocket and carried on ploughing. He worked hard that day, eventually he finished the field and made his way home.

As he was walking along the fields he came upon a rabbit. "Hello rabbit, what have you been up to today?" Bill asked in a friendly manner. The rabbit didn't answer of course, because rabbits can't talk. It just scurried away under the hedge row.

Farmer Jacobs knew that rabbit wouldn't be able to understand him but all of us humans sometimes talk to animals.

Farmer Jacobs finally reached his home. He was very hungry. He was always hungry!! He could already smell that meat pie that Mrs Jacobs was cooking for him.

His only child Annabell, spotted her daddy and ran to greet him. She grabbed hold of him and gave him a big kiss. Annabell loved her daddy.

"Hello Pinky? How are you today?" asked farmer Jacobs, giving his daughter a big cuddle.

"I'm very well, thank you daddy," she replied and then she gave him a kiss on his bearded cheek. "Oh that tickles daddy," said Annabell laughingly.

"What have you been doing today, Pinky?" asked farmer Jacobs.

"I've been around the farm talking to the animals, daddy," replied Annabell.

"But they can't understand you daughter, animals can't talk," said farmer Jacobs.

"Oh, I know that, but I don't have anybody to talk to." Annabell lowered her head and was a little bit sad, she sometimes felt very lonely.

Farmer Jacobs gave his daughter a look of understanding and held her hand as they walked towards the farmhouse.

The farm house was very old, it was built in 1962 and had six bedrooms, it was a big spacious house but in some need of repair. Farmer Jacobs never seemed to be able to find the time to do the repairs. He spent all the hours working on his farm and he was always tired when he came home.

Only Annabell, Mr and Mrs Jacobs and a few dogs lived in the large house.

Annabell is a beautiful eight year old girl with blond hair that she likes to tie in a pony tail. She's a bit on the plump side, just like her daddy, she'll lose that as she gets older but her daddy won't unless he goes on a diet!!

Annabell is a very shy and very lonely little girl, she wishes that she could have a brother or sister but it's not possible because there's something very strange about Annabell.

Mr and Mrs Jacobs tried for years to have a baby but nothing happened. After extensive tests, it was found that Mr Jacobs was sterile. It wasn't possible for him to be able to ever father a baby. But one day against everything the doctors had said, Mrs Jacobs became pregnant. Mr Jacobs was *flabbergasted.* He wondered how the doctors could have made such a mistake.

He couldn't believe what was happening and found it hard to accept that after all the years of knowing that he would never father a child, his wife was suddenly going to have one. Mr Jacobs wasn't sure how this was possible. He insisted on being tested again.

The doctors also thought that they had made a mistake and summoned Mr Jacobs to the hospital to be re-tested but after further testing it was confirmed that they hadn't made a mistake. Mr Jacobs was in fact still sterile, and it was proved that he could not possibly have been the father of the baby.

Mr Jacobs was shocked and was very un-happy. He thought that his wife had strayed and had gone with somebody else but Mrs Jacobs insisted that she hadn't.

Over the next few weeks, the relationship between Mr and Mrs Jacobs became very tense. Mr Jacobs couldn't get it out of his mind. He kept on thinking to himself. If he wasn't the father and he knew that he wasn't, then who was? It was tearing him apart.

He loved his wife more than anything and hated feeling like this. He rowed every day with Mrs Jacobs. He started to lose weight with the worry of it all, but no matter what he said to her, she never wavered.

"The baby is yours husband," she told him. "Why do you not believe me?" But Mr Jacobs didn't believe her, and neither did the people of their village. The gossiping had already started, people that used to be their friends started to distance themselves from the Jacobs.

News travelled through the village about Mrs Jacobs' mysterious pregnancy. Everybody knew that

Bill Jacobs couldn't father a baby, so whose baby was it? No wife or girlfriend in the village trusted their partners now.

Mrs Jacobs was called terrible names by the village people, especially the older women.

It was a very Christian-believing village. Everybody went to church on a Sunday. The only exceptions being Mr Jacobs and Mrs Jacobs.

The priests had banned them. "Not fit to step in the house of God," said one of them. This made Mr Jacobs very, very unhappy.

He loved the church and the people, and strongly believed in God.

It all became too much for him and one day he broke down in tears. He became inconsolable and didn't want to carry on living the life that he was now living.

He shouted at Mrs Jacobs, "It's all your fault, get rid of that *thing* that you've got - it's not mine, I don't want anything to do with it, if you don't get rid of that *thing*, then I'll get rid of you!!" He raged at her!!

This wasn't like Mr Jacobs. It was like the Devil was talking!! In his normal self Mr Jacobs was a wonderful kind man.

The anger within him had unleashed something very evil!! He'd never had a row in his life with Mrs Jacobs, and here he was now hating her. This is the woman that he really loves!!

He didn't want to say these nasty words to her but it was like he'd become *possessed.*

One day it all became too much for him. He ran to his bedroom ranting and raving and eventually cried himself to sleep.

Mrs Jacobs was distraught and was at her wits' end. She loved Mr Jacobs very much, but this wasn't the man that she had married. He'd turned into some kind of *fiend.* She felt that she hadn't done anything wrong. It was his baby but no matter what she said he wouldn't listen to her.

That night Mr Jacobs had what he thought was a dream that would change him. He dreamt that an angel flew down from the heavens. She was beautiful. Her hair was golden and her eyes were a striking sky blue colour that sparkled like the stars at night.

The angel's skin was red!! She was the most beautiful and perfect woman that Mr Jacobs had ever seen. When she spoke her voice was like a beautiful melodic soft tune. The angel was like a rainbow that had fallen out of the sky.

"I've been sent to you sir," said the angel. "You're unhappy, and it's not your fault. Do you believe in God sir?"

"Yes of course I do," replied Mr Jacobs. "Why do you ask? And who are you?"

"It doesn't matter who I am," said the angel. "What matters is, what you are sir. If you believe in God, then God believes in you."

In the angel's arms was a golden shawl which was glowing with the most incredible light, like the sun itself. The angel placed the shawl in the arms of Mr Jacobs.

"Here!" she said. "I've come to show you this baby."

Mr Jacobs opened up the golden shawl to reveal a beautiful baby girl, she looked like the angel!! "Who is she?" asked Mr Jacobs. "She's so beautiful."

"This is your baby to be sir," said the angel. "Do you wish her not to be here?"

"Of course, I do not wish her to be here," said Mr Jacobs angrily. "Why would you say such a horrible thing? A baby is the most precious gift a man can be given. Why would I wish for her not to be here? Why did you say that?"

"But did you not tell your wife yesterday to 'Get rid of that *thing* that you've got'. You called this beautiful baby a *thing*, didn't you sir?"

Mr Jacobs held his head down in shame. "But...but," He could not get the words out of his mouth because he knew that the angel was right.

"There can be no 'buts'," said the angel. "There's no excuse for your behaviour, you are the father of this baby sir - you have been chosen to be her Earth father."

"What do you mean?" said Mr Jacobs, "That I'm her 'Earth father'?"

The angel replied, "It means sir, whatever you think that it means."

"But that's not an answer, all men that live on the Earth that have a child will be their Earth father, whatever else could they be?"

"That's right!" replied the angel. "And you are the father of this baby sir. You must promise to look after her, because she's a very, very special baby. She's the most precious baby the Earth will ever know."

"What do you mean that she is *special*. Why is she special?"

"That I cannot tell you sir - only time will reveal what she will become. Do you promise me, sir that you will love this baby as your own? For she is also the baby of the Almighty!"

Mr Jacobs looked down at the baby girl that was in his arms, and wept with joy.

He held her tiny hand in his - instantly he felt a surge of the most incredible feelings of love go through his body that was being generated by this tiny soul. A bond was formed between them instantly. Mr Jacobs now felt at incredible peace within himself.

"Yes!" he yelled. "I love this baby - I can feel that she's mine." He yelled with great joy.

"Then my task has been fulfilled." The angel picked up the baby from Mr Jacobs' arms and held her up to the heavens. There was a *flash* of bright light and then the baby was gone.

"Hold out your hand sir?" said the angel whose whole body was now glowing.

Mr Jacobs held out his right hand and the angel touched it with hers and then she disappeared in flash of light.

Mr Jacobs yelled, "Please come back - please come back. I want my baby. I love my baby-I love my baby-please bring her back-please come back."

Mrs Jacobs woke up with a fright and wondered what was wrong with Mr Jacobs.

"Husband, what is wrong with you? Are you having a nightmare?"

Mr Jacobs sat up, tears were cascading down his cheeks and were soaking into his beard.

"Oh wife, my beautiful wife. I'm so sorry for what I have said to you," and he grabbed hold of her in a loving embrace and gave her a big kiss on her lips - and then he put his hand upon her stomach. "I love you baby," he said in a soft voice. "You're my baby, and you're so beautiful." He then kissed Mrs Jacob's stomach. "Oh that tickles, husband," said Mrs Jacobs laughing.

Mrs Jacobs was so pleased by her husband's sudden and dramatic change towards her and the baby, but she was baffled as to what had brought about this change in him.

"Husband what has happened to you? You're not the same man that was here with me yesterday."

"I...I.. saw an angel, I think, wife?... She must have been an angel... Yes, that's what she was. She showed me the baby."

He then wiped away a tear drop that was running down his cheek and gave a little sniff. "She's so beautiful, I can't wait for her to be here."

"But how do you know that I'm having a baby girl?" asked Mrs Jacobs taking a little nibble from her finger nail! "Nobody knows what gender the baby is, husband."

"Because, wife, I've seen her!" he yelled out loud. "I'm the happiest man in the whole world!" And then Mr Jacobs started jumping up and down and danced around the room, like he was mad.

Mrs Jacobs started nibbling the next finger on her hand, she was nibbling her finger nails because she couldn't understand what her husband was talking about. None of what he was saying made any sense.

She then took a deep breath of air before she spoke.

"This is not possible husband, how could you have *seen her*?" said Mrs Jacobs in a stern but friendly voice. "She hasn't been born yet. You were only dreaming husband - it was only a dream."

Mrs Jacobs was shaking her head in disbelief at her husband's revelation.

Mr Jacobs could not control his feelings. The baby's touch was still inside his heart.

He spoke softly now. "I have seen her; I have wife, I have; she's very special, please believe me. The angel told me that she's going to be the most special baby the Earth will ever see."

Mrs Jacobs didn't really understand what had brought the change in her husband, but she was very relieved that this kind gentle man was now back to himself even though she felt that he was rambling total nonsense.

From that day on the relationship between them was never better, they were very much in love and couldn't wait for the baby to be born. The months waiting for the baby to arrive seemed like years.

Chapter Two
The Birth of Annabell

Eight months passed and on the ninth of March at 4:30pm (Mr Jacobs' birthday). The baby girl was born on Earth. The birth went well: mother was fine but something was very wrong with the baby.

The doctor and midwife present at the birth couldn't believe what they were seeing. Specialists on the birth of new born babies were urgently summoned. The ward where Annabell was born was isolated. All the other babies were moved out because they thought that Annabell had some strange disease that was not medically known.

The baby appeared to be healthy, but she was born with red coloured skin!! She had one strand of golden hair, and sky blue eyes that sparkled like stars.

Such a baby had never been born on the Earth before - she was unique.

Mr Jacobs was so proud. While everybody else around him was worried about the appearance of the baby he wasn't, because he'd already seen what she looked like eight months previously. She looked exactly like the angel that he'd seen. He couldn't resist touching the baby's hand. Immediately his hand began to tingle. He looked down and was shocked to see an imprint of a star, and the star was shining on his hand!

"Look wife, look at this." He showed her the glowing star that was on his right hand.

"This is the hand that the angel touched," said Mr Jacobs, looking astonished.

"It wasn't a dream wife - it was real! I did see the angel, and I did see our baby. I told you that I did."

The glowing star on Mr Jacobs' hand slowly faded away.

Mrs Jacobs was shocked and baffled by the whole affair. She now knew that her husband had been telling the truth about seeing the baby before.

She certainly was a strange looking baby but Emily Jacobs loved Annabell, and didn't care what she looked like.

DNA samples were taken from Annabell and Mr Jacobs and it was proved beyond any doubt that she was the daughter of Mr Jacobs.

No explanation for this incredible birth could be found. Doctors, and the cleverest scientists in the world, were completely baffled as to how Mr Jacobs could father a child while he was medically diagnosed as sterile, this would be impossible, and nobody could find the reason why Annabell was born the way that she was.

*

The years passed, Annabell was really looking forward to going to school, but on her first day she had to be taken out of the classroom because all her classmates were frightened of her! Nobody would sit next to her and they called her names like, '*The devil child*' because of the red colour of her skin.

It was decided that it would be in the best interest of the school that Annabell left, she was too much of a distraction to the other children. She would have to be schooled at home.

*

Annabell is now eight years old and she is sitting at the table with her parents having her dinner.

Farmer Jacobs finished his dinner, and then remembered the strange object that he had found.

"Emily, look what I found in the field today." He showed his wife the object.

"It's only a stone, husband," said Mrs Jacobs, with not much enthusiasm.

"No wife, it's not a stone, it's some kind of metal. Look at the strange shape that it is? It looks like a quarter of a circle, don't you think? It's got a hole at the narrow end. I wonder if there are any other pieces? I looked for them but I couldn't find any."

"Oh it's only rubbish dear, throw it away, it's not worth anything," said Mrs Jacobs taking away the empty dinner plates from the table.

Annabell was drawn to the object and asked her daddy if she could have a look at it.

Mr Jacobs handed her the object across the dinner table.

Annabell held out her hand and grabbed the object. "OUCH!" she yelled and dropped the object onto the table - it appeared to glow for a split second.

Annabell had felt a strange surge of energy go through her body, like she had got an electric shock.

"Wow! Daddy!" she shrieked.

"What's the matter daughter?" Mr Jacobs looked at his daughter strangely.

"Daddy, it gave me a sort of electric shock when I touched it," said Annabell rubbing her hand.

Mr Jacobs thought that he had seen the object glow but he couldn't understand how that could be, so he dismissed it.

"No, daughter that's not possible," said Mr Jacobs. "You wouldn't get a shock from that, you must have imagined it." But Mr Jacobs did have his doubts because he did think that he saw something.

"No daddy, I didn't," replied Annabell. "It really did give me a shock."

Farmer Jacobs picked up the object from the table and held it in his hand and squeezed it tightly. He felt nothing, and the object didn't glow.

"See daughter, it couldn't have given you a shock. It's only a piece of metal."

Annabell was reassured by her father's demonstration and asked him if she could have it.

"Yeah, I don't see why not," said farmer Jacobs. "I'll see if I can find that old gold chain necklace that was in the drawer that your nanny gave to me, I'll put it on that."

Farmer Jacobs searched through a drawer in the sitting room and came across the gold chain. He placed the chain through the hole that was in the object and put it around the neck of Annabell, and then he went out of the room to have a cup of tea in the sitting room with Mrs Jacobs.

Instantly, Annabell felt a strong surge of energy go through her whole body. The object began to glow around her neck. The object was constantly changing colours. One minute it was red, then blue, then yellow; it was changing to every colour of the rainbow.

Annabell was very excited by this, the surge of energy didn't hurt her, she couldn't wait to tell her parents what was happening.

She ran to the sitting room and opened the door.

The two dogs rushed passed her nearly knocking her over. The dogs were farmer Jacobs' sheep dogs, named Bonnie and Chrissie.

Annabell shouted at the dogs. "Be careful!" she said with a frown on her face. "You nearly knocked me over, Bonnie."

"Oh, I'm sorry Annabell," replied Bonnie.

"What?" Annabell was aghast, " Err...did you just talk, Bonnie?"

"Yes," answered the dog like it was a perfectly natural thing to do.

"I can talk as well," said Chrissie, jumping up and down excitedly.

"But-but…b-but…animals can't talk." Annabell was stunned and shocked.

" Err…um…" She couldn't get the words out of her mouth. "But-but… h-how is that possible?" Annabell was stuttering her words.

"We don't know," both the dogs answered together. "We've never been able to understand humans before," said Chrissie. "We knew about the sounds that farmer Jacobs has taught us…like "Stop" "Go" and…" Sit," but that's about all."

Annabell was so excited. "Mummy. Daddy come here quickly," she shouted at the top of her voice. "Quick…quickly"

Mr and Mrs Jacobs rushed out the room that they were in with great anxiety.

"What's wrong daughter, are you hurt?" asked farmer Jacobs. They were both very concerned.

"No, no, mummy, daddy. I need to tell you something important. Very important."

"What is it darling?" asked Mrs Jacobs.

Annabell rushed the words out of her mouth as fast as she could. "Bonnie and Chrissie can talk!" she shrieked.

"Oh, Pinky, don't be so silly," said farmer Jacobs, with a smile on his face. "Animals can't talk darling."

"But, they can," answered Annabell, excitedly. "Listen to this," Annabell turned to Bonnie.

"What's my name?" Annabell was gesturing with her hands for Bonnie to give her the answer.

"Your name is Annabell, but your daddy calls you Pinky sometimes," said Bonnie.

"There! What did I tell you, I told you they could talk," said Annabell with a broad smile on her face.

Farmer Jacobs and Mrs Jacobs, just stood there for a few moments and looked at each other dumbfounded, and they laughed.

"But daughter the dog just said, Woof...woff... woff...woff." And farmer Jacobs laughed out loud and cuddled his daughter.

"No daddy, you're wrong...mummy tell him, you heard Bonnie speak, didn't you?"

Mrs Jacobs shook her head. "No Annabell, the dog, just went 'woof'! That's all dogs can do, they can't do anything else."

"But; I heard her say my name, mummy. She knew my real name is Annabell."

"Chrissie, what did you do today? Tell my mummy and daddy."

" I went out in the fields and rounded up the sheep for farmer Jacobs," said Chrissie.

"There! You must have heard that, see I told you they can talk." Annabell felt really pleased with herself for being right.

" No daughter the dog didn't talk. It just went. Woof...woof...woof...woof...woof."

Annabell was getting very agitated. "But...but - oh, why can't you hear them speak? Bonnie: Chrissie, why can't my mummy and daddy hear you talk?"

The two dogs nodded their heads and said or *woofed* in the case of farmer Jacobs and Mrs Jacobs.

"We don't know. We can't understand what they're saying either, it's just noises to us. We can understand you though."

Suddenly Mrs Jacobs caught sight of Annabell's necklace. "**My God!**" she screamed. "The stone thing is on fire! Quick! get it off, it may explode!"

Fearing for the safety of her daughter Mrs Jacobs snatched the necklace off Annabell's neck breaking the chain. She threw it out of the window.

Annabell started to cry. "Mummy, mummy. I love my necklace, it didn't hurt me, please may I have it back?" she sobbed.

The two dogs started howling and barking with all the commotion that was going on.

"Be quite, Bonnie and Chrissie," Annabell yelled, and then she carried on sobbing.

The two dogs took no notice of Annabell and carried on barking.

"Bonnie, will you shut up please," Annabell screamed. She was still upset about the necklace.

Bonnie didn't respond. "Don't you understand me?" yelled Annabell.

There was no reply from the dogs. It appeared that the dogs could no longer speak or understand Annabell.

Then they started scratching at the door trying to get out. They were going crazy! They made deep scratch marks down the side of the door. Farmer Jacobs quickly opened the door and let the two dogs out. They both rushed out of the house as fast as they could go.

A few minutes later Bonnie came back with the necklace holding the object in her jaws. She dropped it at the feet of Annabell. The object was no longer glowing, it was just a drab grey colour.

Mrs Jacobs rushed over to the necklace before Annabell could pick it up, and she threw it even harder out of the window. The necklace went high into the air before landing somewhere behind a bush at the back of the farmhouse.

But once again Bonnie rushed out of the house and brought it back. Farmer Jacobs tried to get the necklace out of the jaws of Bonnie, but she wouldn't let it go. The more he pulled the more she pulled back. In the end he gave up. Then Bonnie calmly placed the necklace down at the feet of Annabell.

Farmer Jacobs went to pick it up, but the two dogs started growling at him. He pushed both dogs out of the room and picked up the necklace. Mrs Jacobs told her husband to get rid of it.

Farmer Jacobs went straight to his work shop that was located in a building a short distance from the main house. He undid the chains clip to take the object off the necklace. Strangely the necklace chain was no longer broken.

When Mrs Jacobs pulled it off Annabell's neck she definitely broke the chain but somehow the chain had repaired itself.

Mr Jacobs placed the object on an anvil. He then started hitting it with a great big hammer! But it made no impression whatsoever on the object. He got a bigger hammer but it made no difference it didn't even scratch it. He was getting very frustrated.

He lit his furnace. When the furnace was as hot as it could get Farmer Jacobs threw the object into it and heaped the coal around it to form a mound. This he thought would melt the object. When the furnace had cooled down farmer Jacobs searched through the ashes not expecting to find anything. But to his shock and horror the object was intact!

In desperation he put it into a bowl of acid, and left it overnight but when he looked at it in the morning the object was exactly the same. It now appeared that whatever this object was, it seemed to be indestructible.

The next day Farmer Jacobs got on his tractor and drove to one of his fields that was over a mile away from his house. He dug a deep hole at least six feet deep! And placed the object in a metal box. He put it at the bottom of the hole, and placed rocks over the top of it and then covered it over with soil. He then put an extra layer of rocks on top.

When he arrived home he told Mrs Jacobs that he'd got rid of it for good.

*

Several months passed the object was forgotten about. Mr Jacobs gave Annabell back the gold necklace which she wore. Over the months no matter how hard Annabell tried she could never get those dogs to talk again.

Annabell had become very upset because one of the dogs, Bonnie had gone missing. She hadn't been seen for over a week. Mr Jacobs had been going out every day on the farm looking for her.

Then one early morning Annabell heard scratching at her bedroom door.

Annabell had been asleep she was a bit annoyed. She thought that it was Chrissie trying to get into her room so that she could sleep on her bed, which she did quite often.

Annabell got out of bed and opened the door. She screamed! Bonnie was sitting there, she was covered in mud, and her mouth and paws were bleeding. Annabell noticed that Bonnie had something in her mouth, She opened it up, and inside was the object that Mr Jacobs had tried to hide several months ago but Bonnie had found it!

Annabell had the object in her hand. Instantly she felt a tremendous surge of energy go through her body and the object lit up using all the colours of the rainbow. She put the object back on her necklace and fastened it around her neck - Annabell took Bonnie downstairs and cleaned her up and fed her. She soon recovered.

Annabell was so excited to get the object back. She ran out of the house like a naughty little girl that has done something wrong.

She ran straight down to her favourite horse, whose name is Charlie.

"Morning Charlie. Look at the lovely charm on my necklace that my daddy found, do you like it?"

"Yes I do," replied the horse.

"You can talk?" shrieked Annabell.

"Yes," said Charlie.

Annabell was so happy she realised now that it was the object that possessed magic powers.

"Charlie it's magic! This is how I can talk to you. I have a magic necklace. Wow! This is so exciting," she yelled.

Annabell was now able to understand all of the animals, and any living creature, as long as she wore her necklace containing the magic object.

Over the next few weeks she went around the farm every day talking to the animals and gave them all names. What fun she was having with all her animal friends. She had more friends than anyone in the whole world.

There was a family of ducks living on the farm pond, whom she named Mr & Mrs Jones. There were lots of other ducks living on the pond, but they were all single. There were boys and girls but they were too young to get married.

Her best friends were, Charlie the horse and Ronald the bull. Ronald had loads of wives! In the animal world he was allowed to do this. Annabell couldn't remember all his wives' names there were far too many of them. Ronald used to try and hide from them so that he could get some peace and quiet from their nagging! but they always found him! He asked Annabell if she could find him a field so that he could be by himself for a while. He told her that he needed some rest. Ronald had fathered hundreds of babies over the years.

Annabell used to have fun with Ronald and sometimes she would tell his wives where he was just to annoy him. Ronald was not amused by Annabell's antics but sometimes she would put him in with Charlie the horse so that he could get away from them.

Ronald really loved all his wives, but he just had too many of them to cope with.

There was also a family of pigeons living in the big old oak tree that was near the farmhouse. Annabell named them Mr & Mrs Dawn, She named them this because they always woke her up at dawn! With their *'cooing'!*

The Dawns had been busy over the last few weeks making a nest. Mrs Dawn had laid six eggs. Pretty soon she and Mr Dawn would hopefully have six new babies.

Annabell checked every day to see if the babies were born. She was really looking forward to seeing them.

Annabell was such a happy child now that she had so many friends.

Farmer Jacobs & Mrs Jacobs had seen a big change in their daughter, they were so pleased to see her so happy. But little did they know the real reason for her happiness.

Months and months went by. Farmer Jacobs carried on with his farm work. Mr & Mrs Dawn had their babies. The incident with the necklace was never mentioned again. Farmer Jacobs and Mrs Jacobs had no idea that their daughter was wearing the necklace. She kept it hidden and only wore it when her mummy and daddy couldn't see her.

Chapter Three
Annabell's Abduction

Every morning before her schooling she would come out to speak to all her animal friends. But one day when she was talking to Ronald the bull, Annabell could see something very strange flying, way in the distance. It wasn't a plane, it looked a bit like a bird! But it was huge! It had massive wings, each wing was at least thirteen feet wide. Annabell stood rooted to the spot. "What is it Ronald?" she asked in a very frightened voice.

"What's what?" Ronald couldn't see anything.

Annabell pointed to what she was seeing but Ronald couldn't see anything.

"I've never seen anything like it, Ronald. Wow! can't you see that big bird?"

"No!" said Ronald looking puzzled.

"But it's huge! Look at the size of those wings. Whatever is it, it's coming this way." Annabell ran as fast as she could to try and get to the safety of the farmhouse. Whatever it was, was getting closer and closer to Annabell. It seemed to be coming right at her.

She could see it clearly now. It was a giant bird of some kind but nothing of the like that she'd ever seen before.

It had a strange head with a triangular crest on top. And it had a long slender beak and claw like feet.

The huge bird was coming down fast, Annabell could hear the swishing noise of its wings as it was getting closer all the time.

Annabell ran as fast as she could. She was screaming as loud as she could. **"Mummy! Daddy! Help! Help!"** She nearly reached the front door, but was just too late. The big bird swooped down and picked up Annabell with its huge spiky feet, it flapped its giant wings and took her away from the farm.

Annabell was screaming and kicking. She was trying to punch the bird, but it wouldn't let her go. She became hysterical and was crying for help but nobody could help her.

The big bird flew high in the sky with Annabell dangling. If the bird would have dropped her now she would have been killed by the fall for sure.

The bird flew for several miles until it reached a forest, where it placed Annabell very gently on the ground.

Annabell was so frightened. "Please - please, don't eat me," she pleaded. "I'm only a little girl, I'm only eight years old, I don't want to be eaten." And then she started to cry, "I want my mummy and daddy."

"I won't eat you," said the big bird. "Please calm down, Annabell. I'm really sorry that I frightened you but I had no choice, I need your help, it's a matter of life and death!"

Annabell was relieved that the bird wasn't hostile and that she could talk to it. She breathed a sigh of relief that it wasn't going to eat her.

"I don't understand," said Annabell. "I've never been so scared in all my life - I thought that I was going to die! You know what? I don't mean to be unkind, but you're the ugliest bird that I've ever seen." With those words, she kicked the big bird.

"How dare you do that to me, take me home right now. I want my mummy. My dad has got a big stick and if he would have seen you take me, he would have tried to bash you with it, and maybe we would have eaten you for our dinner!"

The big bird scampered away, he was a bit shocked that Annabell had kicked him, and he really didn't think that anybody would want to eat him.

"OUCH!" he said, hopping on one leg. "That hurt!"

"Good!" replied Annabell, with a grin on her face. She liked that. She felt like she had got a little bit of her own back on the bird "And… if you come near me again, I'll kick you again!" said Annabell sternly.

"Sorry! Sorry! Annabell," said the big bird. The big bird was more frightened of her than she was of him now.

"Annabell listen to me, we haven't got much time. I need your help, I've travelled time to find you."

Annabell put her hands on her hips and said with an air of authority. "You need my help? And you've travelled through time to find me, well, you've wasted your time!" Annabell laughed "I can't help you, I'm only a little girl, I'm only eight years old you know, and how do you know my name?"

" Because I do," said the bird still hopping on one leg. "You have powers Annabell. I've been guided here to find you," said the bird flapping it's giant wings.

"But...but...I don't have any powers. I don't know what you're talking about," said Annabell nodding her head. "You've wasted your time."

"Yes, you do have powers; you know you have," said the bird. "You have the power of the land seed, see how it glows on you! You're the only person in the whole world that the land object will work for, you're *unique*, a one off, you're a very special person.

"Look at yourself, you're different from other people, look at the colour of your skin. Nobody in the world is like you. There has never been anybody like you, in...well millions of years... In fact, never!" said the bird and he repeated himself. "*Never!*"

Annabell knew that the bird was correct, she knew that she was different to other people.

"Will you help us, Annabell?" pleaded the bird.

"Us?...Who's us?"

"I can't tell you that yet," said the bird mysteriously. "But please trust me, I'm begging you; please say yes - it's very important, it will be the most memorable thing that you will do in your whole life, you will never be forgotten, what you will be asked to do, will have a change on the world. That's all that I can tell you."

Annabell thought about what the big bird had said.

"It's a matter of life and death." She knew that she couldn't refuse.

"Big bird, what about my mummy and daddy? They're going to be so worried about me. I'm not allowed to stay out at night by myself and it's getting nearly dark. They will call the police you know. The police don't take too kindly to people who kidnap children. It's against the law: it's a very serious offence, it's called kid-nap-ping."

" Yes, I know it is," said the bird. "But I'm not a person, so the law doesn't apply to me, I'm sorry to kidnap you, I really am, but I had no choice, and nobody would understand where we're about to go. You must try and be brave and trust me, your mummy and daddy and the world will be so proud of you when you return."

"Oh, ok, alright," she blurted out. "Yeah, alright then, I will help you. My mummy and daddy have always taught me, that I must be a good person even when people make fun of me, they always say to me that it's just that they don't understand, because I'm not like them."

The big bird bent down and gave Annabell a peck on her cheek. "Thank you! You're a kind little girl and you're very beautiful; and I don't mind you calling me *'ugly'.* To my wife and children, I'm beautiful!"

"Oh," said Annabell realising that what she had said to the bird is what people had said about her.

"I'm sorry big bird, that wasn't a nice thing for me to say, and I'm sorry that I kicked you! Well a little bit sorry, I think that you deserved it though. What you did to me was horrible, making me dangle in the sky. Anyway what kind of bird are you? The biggest bird that I've ever seen is an ostrich. It's the biggest bird in the whole world, I've read all about it in my school books, but it can't fly. You're...um, you're, um, five: no, ten...times bigger than that bird and you can fly. What are you? And where did you come from?"

The big bird looked at Annabell . " If I told you, you wouldn't believe it - so I won't tell what kind of bird that I am. It's best if I don't, I think," said the bird not really knowing.

"But...um!" Annabell was about to say something.

"Annabell don't bother, believe me, you won't understand," said the bird.

" Well, what's your name then? I need to have your name, I can't just call you big bird."

"My name is Bambalata," said the bird.

"Bambalata? That's a lovely name, I like that," said Annabell smiling.

"Oh, I'm really hungry Bambalata." Annabell rubbed her tummy. "Have you got anything to eat? I get very moody if I don't eat."

Bambalata flew off and told Annabell that he wouldn't be long.

He was gone for at least forty minutes though. When he returned, he had in his clasp a bowl, that he had made from leaves and small twigs that he had found in the forest.

He handed the bowl to Annabell. "Here's some food," he said, *proudly.* "Enjoy!"

Annabell thanked Bambalata, she couldn't wait to tuck into her meal.

"What have you brought me? I hope that it's something nice. I'm *starving*! I could eat a *horse*!" she said, joking.

She tipped the contents of the bowl out onto her lap, she was sitting down on the ground at the time. Out of the bowl fell Apples, Plums, Blackberries, Worms! Caterpillars! Flies! And half a fish! Which may have been a minnow.

Annabell *Screamed* and stood up on her feet as fast as she could, and shook all the food off her dress. "ARRGH!...ARRGH!...ARRRGH!... What's this? ARGH!... ARGH!..."

She was jumping up and down *screaming* with her hands moving as fast as possible trying to brush the rest of the bugs off her dress.

Bambalata just stood there making a bird laughing sort of noise. "What's the matter with you?" He was baffled as to what was the matter with her.

"Bambalata," she *shrieked.* "Get all these creepy crawlies away from me, **NOW!**" And I mean right now!" She continued jumping up and down with her hands now holding her dress down.

"What is wrong with you? Don't you like my food?" asked Bambalata.

"NO, I DON'T!" she screamed.

Bambalata was a bit miffed. "I thought that you said you was *hungry*?"

"I am hungry," yelled Annabell. "But I'm not eating *BUGS* for God's sake! Bambalata, why did you bring me bugs? That's not food."

"What's wrong with my food? I thought that you would like it. I've caught for you the very fattest and juiciest worms, caterpillars and look at those flies, hmmm! lovely. It's a feast, isn't it?"

"NO!" she *screamed.* *"*It isn't a *feast!* It's horrible! I don't eat bugs! And you'd better not eat those things when you're near me! I'll be sick if you do."

Bambalata really thought that he had brought Annabell a feast. To him it was, it's what he ate, but he had made a big mistake of not asking what she ate.

Bambalata picked up all the bugs from the ground and put them back into the bowl.

Annabell *yelled* out again. "BAMBALATA, get those horrible bugs away from me."

"Alright! Alright! You ungrateful little girl. I had to work really hard to find this lovely food for you, if you don't want it, I'll eat it myself...hmm! Just look at those gorgeous caterpillars! They're my favourite. They're so juicy."

Bambalata did what he was told and moved away from Annabell and went behind a tree so that she couldn't see him eating. Ten minutes later he returned, licking his lips with his huge tongue. "Ah! they were delicious, I'm really full up now."

Bambalata had obviously enjoyed his meal, he had bug juice dribbling down the side of his beak and the remains of a fly wing was jutting out!

"Errrrrrrr! You're the most disgusting bird thing ever Bambalata... you know that? Why don't you wipe your mouth? Or beak! Or whatever you call it? My mummy said that I should always wipe my mouth after my meal. Please wipe your beak - mouth? - thing? You're making me feel very sick."

Annabell ran into the bushes and pretended to be sick. Bambalata got the message and wiped his beak.

"You need to eat some food Annabell, we've got a long way to go. I'm sorry that you didn't like my food, if you tell me what you like I'll see if I can find it for you."

Annabell said in a *loud* voice. "I eat Hamburgers, Chicken nuggets, Bacon and Eggs. I like everything with fries. Yummy! especially, steak. Can you get me, steak double egg and fries with tomato sauce? Please."

"What kind of food is this?" asked Bambalata with a somewhat puzzled look on his face. "If you describe it, I'll see if I can catch it for you."

Bambalata was trying his best to help, but he really didn't understand what Annabell was talking about.

"Don't be so silly Bambalata! You can't *catch it.* Mummy buys it from a supermarket and takes it home and then she cooks it - but sometimes we go out to a fast food restaurant where other people cook it for you."

Bambalata looked at Annabell for several moments before speaking. "What does *buy* mean? and what's a 'fast food restaurant'? If I knew what they mean, I might be able to get your food for you."

Annabell gave out a big sigh. "Oh, how I wish Bambalata; how I wish - but you can't buy my food in a forest! And I think that if you went into the shops to try and buy it, I don't think that you'll be served." Annabell started to laugh loudly.

She realised that she wasn't going to get any food and she was getting to the stage when she wouldn't want to eat anything that Bambalata brought to her anyway. In desperation, she picked up an apple from the ground, wiped it down the side of her dress.

"Oh, I suppose it'll be alright to eat this apple," she said to herself. It was a nice big apple and looked very inviting, especially when she was so hungry. Annabell's mouth was watering and she dribbled in anticipation of the meal. Bambalata noticed this and just had to say something.

"What's that dribbling down the side of your mouth? You're disgusting Annabell!" Then he laughed out loud.

She didn't say anything, all she could see was this big juicy apple. She opened her mouth as wide as she could showing off her beautiful set of perfect teeth. She bit off the biggest chunk that was possible for her to bite and started chewing.

It was a lovely flavoured apple. With her mouth full, she somehow managed to blurt out the words that could have said, "This is nice!" but it was only a guess, because whatever she said didn't sound remotely like the English language!

She chewed and chewed, but no matter how much she chewed she couldn't seem to be able to finish the piece of apple that she had bitten off, and it got more and more chewy! In the end she had to give up. She put her thumb and finger to her mouth and pulled out the remains of the apple but it wasn't the apple that she had been chewing. it was a big bug! And it was now lying *limp* on her finger. Annabell screamed and then she flicked it at Bambalata in a fit of temper, hitting him between his eyes!

The chewed bug slid down his face towards his mouth. His big tongue whipped out so fast and grabbed the bug and he gobbled it up! " Mmmm… That was nice; thanks!" he said gratefully.

Annabell was not amused. "You are without any doubt the most disgusting creature that has ever… and I mean, **ever** lived, Bambalata. I can't eat anything without there being a bug involved." Annabell was stamping her feet into the ground and then she started spitting out the juices from her mouth, she knew that this was not ladylike but she didn't care at this moment in time. This was an emergency situation. The rules didn't count. "What are you trying to do to me, Bambalata : poison me or something?"

Annabell threw the rest of the apple in a raging temper. It hit a nearby tree and splattered all over Bambalata's head. "Ah!" he said smiling. *"Pudding!* What's the matter with you now, you moaning little girl!"

"What's the matter with me? BUGS! … BUGS!… BUGS!… and I've just eaten one in your nasty apple. That's what's the matter with me."

"I knew that there was a 'bug' as you call them, in the apple.." said Bambalata. That's why I picked it. These are very special apples you know. It's not easy finding them, you have to be skilled to spot one - it's a hundred to one chance of finding one and I found you three bug apples!!!"

"I could really dislike you sometimes, Bambalata, I really could. Why didn't you tell me that there was a bug in the apple?"

"Because my moaning little girl you didn't ask! So I didn't tell you, anyway it was fun. I've never had so much fun in all my life."

"I'll tell you something, Bambalata, I'm not eating anymore of your rotten food, I'd rather starve!"

Annabell sat under a tree with a frown on her face and refused to speak to him. Bambalata didn't mind he was glad to have some peace and quiet, he had a lot of work to do anyway.

After his meal Bambalata started work on making a nest, so that Annabell could sit in it and be more comfortable for her long journey ahead.

He laboured for hours in the forest gathering up the bits that he needed. At last, he finally finished it. It was a wonderful nest made in two halves.

"Come on Annabell we haven't got much time. Please get into the nest."

She reluctantly clambered over the side of the nest and fell inside and landed on her back, with her legs outstretched in the air!

"You could have helped me get inside, Bambalata," she moaned.

Bambalata didn't say anything. He tied the top and bottom together, so that she wouldn't fall out and placed leaves inside so that she would be nice and warm. He'd made sort of ropes out of what he found in the forest and connected them to the nest, like a sort of parachute, but upside down. He tied the ropes securely to his huge legs and told Annabell to hold on tightly.

He flapped his giant wings and took off. All that Annabell could hear was WHOSH! - WHOSH! the sound made by the flapping of his huge wings.

Annabell was warm and cosy in her nest and soon fell fast asleep. She slept for hours and hours. Day had turned into night and back to day again. Bamblata had flown non - stop all through the night. Annabell finally woke up feeling very cold, she looked over the top of her nest. In front of her was a big mountain.

Bambalata was flapping his wings frantically trying to gain height. He went higher and higher, it seemed like the mountain was miles high, up and up he went. The weight of the nest was clearly holding him back but you could see the determination in his eyes. He had to reach the top. Annabell thought that this must be the place that her help was needed. The life and death situation must be at this place, but what it was she didn't know.

Chapter Four
Meeting Pete

At last they reached the top of the mountain. Bambalata was absolutely exhausted. He carefully lowered the nest to the ground. He undid the ropes that were tied to his feet and let Annabell get out of the nest. He fell to the ground with an almighty thump and lay motionless with his wings spread out like an aeroplane. Annabell screamed! "What's the matter, Bambalata?" But he didn't say anything. He was sprawled out on the ground not moving. Annabell was really worried, she thought that Bambalata was dead! "Bambalata, please wake up, I don't want you to die...please don't be dead."

She ran over to where his body lay. He was still motionless. Tears were rolling down her face. "Bambalata, I love you... please wake up." Suddenly he opened his big eye and winked at Annabell! "I'm alright, I just went dizzy for a few moments. I'm so tired, I may have passed out but I'm alright now. So you love me, do you?"

Annabell was a bit embarrassed. "I thought that you were dead! How will I get home without you? I was really worried."

"So you don't love me then?" said Bambalata jokingly.

"Well, I suppose I have grown a bit fond of you... you're still ugly though! Only joking! Where are we, Bambalata?"

"We're on top of a mountain, in a jungle, I don't know what they call this country."

"But...why have you brought me here? I need to know." Annabell had so many questions, but wasn't getting any answers. "Why won't you tell me? Bambalata, I demand that you tell me."

"Soon...Annabell ...Soon, you will find out. I'm going to leave you here for the night. I'll pick you up in the morning." Annabell was shocked.

"NO!" she yelled. "You can't leave me here all on my own. I'm only a little girl, I'm not allowed to be on my own."

"You'll be alright Annabell you won't be alone for very long, something will come for you soon, trust me. I really need to rest, we have a long journey tomorrow,

I have to take you back to your home." Bambalata flapped his wings and flew away.

"BAMBALATA ,YOU COME BACK HERE AT ONCE!" Annabell shouted at him.

"If you don't come back right now, I won't be your friend anymore!" But Bambalata was gone.

Annabell was all alone now - it was very quiet and peaceful here. She looked around and couldn't believe her eyes. She was in a very strange place. There were lots of conifers and plants that she had never seen before, but the trees and plants appeared to be dying and there were crystal clear blue coloured lakes. But there were lots of strange looking fish lying dead on top of the water. It was clear that something horrible was happening here.

She was on a huge mountain that didn't actually look like a mountain, because it was flat on top. If a plane was to fly over it, the pilot wouldn't know that it was a mountain. It was like an optical illusion. It was strangely warm on top of this mountain, despite it being sometimes above the clouds. It should have been really cold here. Annabell had noticed that while travelling to this place it had got extremely cold but here it was very warm and pleasant.

She could see loads of caves and there were pathways that led into interesting looking places that went inside the mountain.

Annabell felt very frightened here. She didn't like being on her own in this strange place, maybe thousands of miles away from her mummy and daddy, she knew that they must be going frantic with worry wondering where she was.

Annabell was right. Back at the Jacobs' farm, the police had been called in.

Hundreds of people were searching for her. She'd been missing now for over twenty four hours. The farm was sealed off. Police bulletins were constantly being broadcast on television and radio for anybody to come forward with information regarding any sightings of her.

News people were gathering at the farm. Annabell's disappearance was becoming a big news story. Everybody was very concerned about her. Annabell was already quite famous in America and other parts of the world.

One man came forward and said that he had seen a girl, a *'red girl'!* dangling in the sky and she was flying at great speed. The police cautioned this man for wasting police time with such a ridiculous story and told him to clear off!

The farm was thoroughly searched but no trace of Annabell could be found.

Meanwhile back on the mountain, Annabell started yelling out, "HELLO! Is there anybody here?" She repeated it for several minutes, but there was no response.

It was very quiet and sort of eerie, there wasn't a sound of anything. Annabell just sat there by the lake throwing pebbles into the water just to see the ripples.

The lake was rather strange because it had bubbles coming to the surface of the water. It was like it was starting to boil. Annabell put her hand into the water and it was very warm! She now knew why the fish had died.

The hours passed. Bambalata said that something would come but nothing had.

All the time Annabell felt it was getting warmer and warmer, and the lake was beginning to steam.

Bambalata had said it was a matter of life and death, but there was no life here. She was puzzled why she had been brought here, why wouldn't Bambalata tell her? She pondered about this. What was the secret of this place?

Annabell wished that something would happen soon. She was getting very bored and tired just sitting here doing nothing, and the heat was becoming overpowering.

Several more hours passed. Annabell's eyes started to close, they felt like lead, eventually she couldn't keep them open any longer and she fell fast asleep.

She was having a lovely sleep, when all of a sudden she was woken up by what she thought was the sound of *THUNDER!* She woke up with a bit of a fright. While she was asleep it had become very misty, more like steamy. Annabell couldn't see a thing and it was getting all the time, hotter! And there was a horrible smell!

She could still hear a noise in the distance, but it wasn't thunder, it was more like somebody banging on the ground, THUMP!...THUMP!...THUMP!... and all the time it was getting nearer and louder to her. THUMP!THUMP!...THUMP!...THUMP! Annabell was very frightened now and hid behind a rock. Suddenly the thumping stopped but now she could hear heavy breathing, this frightened her even more. She didn't dare move or make a sound, but the breathing was like a gale force wind, like whistling in -whistle out, whistle in -whistle out, She could hear the pine needles on the trees rustling every time when whatever it was breathed out. She rolled herself up in a ball, just like a hedgehog and closed her eyes.

"Hello Annabell." Whatever it was, knew who she was. "I've been expecting you. Please come out from behind that rock, I know that you're there, I will not harm you, do not be afraid."

But Annabell was afraid, in fact she was frightened out of her life.

Bambalata was bad enough but whatever this was - was even scarier, its voice was so loud that Annabell had to cover her ears, but it was still loud! She was a very brave little girl though. She sneakily, slowly opened one eye. All that she could see was a huge something. It looked like a tree, but it moved! Annabell screamed and yelled out at the top of her voice, "**GET AWAY FROM ME!** I want my mummy and daddy, you'd better go away from me otherwise I'll throw something at you!"

It wasn't a tree, it was a huge leg that she had been looking at and now she could see its foot, it was nearly as big as her! Annabell screamed, "BAMBALATA… BAMBALATA…Where are you? I need your help, there's something horrible here and it's talking to me."

But Bambalata couldn't help her, because he wasn't there.

"Please don't hurt me, I'm only a little girl - I'm only eight years old. I won't be very good to eat! There's not much meat on me." (In fact, there was a lot of meat on her!! She was quite a plump girl for her age.) Annabell was once again pleading for her life. The poor little girl had really been put through a most frightening experience.

"Annabell." Whatever it was spoke again. But although it was a very loud gruff voice, it was kind of gentle at the same time.

"I will not harm you - and I don't eat meat! Bambalata was sent to find you. I need your help, I haven't got much time. Please, will you come out from behind that rock?"

Annabell felt not so afraid now. It said that Bambalata had been sent to find her.

She trusted Bambalata, (well sort of trusted him!) Slowly, very slowly, she moved away from the cover of the rock to face whatever it was that was standing there. The mist or steam had cleared a bit now. She could see a huge creature, it had a really long neck and its tail stretched way in the distance. She looked up - and up - and up, her neck was bent right back to the full and still she couldn't see its head! Annabell walked backwards a little bit, until she eventually saw the creature's head. She was a brave little girl.

"WOW!" she yelled. "You're big! You're bigger than my house! What on earth are you?"

"I'm, what your kind has named, a dinosaur. I'm a Brachiosaurus."

"NO - NO- You can't be, I've read books, all about dinosaurs, they say that you're *extinct!* That means you're all dead! And…And…it was millions of years ago. My mummy and daddy took me to a museum once…they've got dinosaur bones there and they're all wired up to make them look real, but they haven't got any skin! In fact, I'm sure that I've seen your bones in there. Brachiosaurus are definitely all extinct. So how come you're alive? My teacher Mrs Grant, who comes to my house to teach me told me that a huge rock hit the Earth millions of years ago and that all dinosaurs were killed. So you can't possibly be a dinosaur...You're telling me fibs. I...I want my mummy and daddy. I miss them and I want to go home now and if you don't take me home, they'll get the police to find you and then you'll be in trouble." Annabell started to cry, it was all getting a bit too much for her. She sobbed and sobbed.

"Please- please don't cry, Annabell I don't want to upset you, I know that you're only a little girl and you're a very, very brave one. I do understand that you miss your mummy and daddy and I promise you that you will see them very soon. But only you can help me, Annabell. You have magic powers! I need you to use the powers that you have to save..." The giant creature didn't finish the sentence, he seemed to not be able to say the last words.

A few moments later he spoke.

"...I have very little time left." The creature seemed to give out a desperate sigh.

Annabell rubbed her eyes and mopped up the tears. "But I don't have the powers; I can only talk to animals I...I...don't know what you're saying. How can I help you? Save you from what? I don't understand. I want my mummy, and daddy. Please take me home. If the police catch you they'll put you in an animal prison.

So you'd better take me home before they catch you. If you don't I'll scream!"

With that Annabell started *screaming* at the top of her voice. Her screams started echoing off the rocks and were now as loud as the giant animal's voice! She couldn't stand the noise herself so she stopped.

"Nobody can hear you," said the giant animal. "There's nobody here, only you and me. Please come with me, Annabell, we haven't got much time."

"Time for what?" asked Annabell with a puzzled look on her face.

Suddenly there was a loud hissing noise coming from a nearby rock, followed by a huge spray of hot steaming water that went high into the air.

" Quick!" said the giant animal despairingly. "We've got to get away from here, you're in danger if we stay here, come Annabell, we must go now."

"What was that?" asked Annabell with a look of astonishment.

"That's a geyser," replied the giant animal.

"But why is hot water coming from the ground? And why is it so hot here? My feet are getting hot."

Suddenly there was a huge explosion over the other side of the mountain. Annabell screamed, "**WHAT WAS THAT?**" And then she could see a massive plume of thick dark smoke in the distance.

"This is a volcanic mountain, Annabell. It's been dormant for years but it's about to erupt again - it will soon explode, maybe only in hours. The Earth got very cold. Most of my kind died through the cold. There was no food for us to eat so I, and a few other dinosaurs came to this mountain that was warm and there was food here. The extreme cold hadn't touched this place so we were saved for quite a few years. The mountain is now contaminated, Annabell, I haven't got much time. This is why I need your help. All my kind are dead now, I'm the last Brachiosaurus. All the food and water is poisonous on this mountain. I too will soon die."

"Why didn't you just come down from this mountain?" asked Annabell. "If you would have got off, you would have lived."

"No! - No! Annabell. It's not only contaminated here on this mountain. This part of the Earth is too cold. The Earth is going through a serious change ,Annabell. The surface is on the move. The crust and the mantle are continually forming and being destroyed. Soon there's going to be a massive change in the plate tectonics that will change the Earth drastically, and it's going to start right here."

The giant animal started to cry. Huge tears were cascading from his eyes and hitting the ground with huge splashes.

Annabell felt very sad for the animal, she too had tears flowing freely from her eyes.

"But how do you know this?" asked Annabell. "What will happen to my family and all the people and animals, we must try and save them."

"No!- no! - You don't understand - it's not in your time, it's in my time. Dinosaurs don't live in your time, Annabell."

Annabell was confused. "What time is your time, and what time is my time?"

The giant animal didn't know how to tell Annabell. "Annabell, this is 145 million years before your time."

"A?" said Annabell. "What? How can it be 145 million years before me? What is the date now in my time, do you even know?"

"2209 Annabell."

"What is your time?"

"145 million years before 2209."

"But how can I travel 145 million years in the past? And how do you know about what's going to happen, if it hasn't happened yet?"

"I really don't know, Annabell, but I believe that it has something to do with that object that's around your neck. Believe me, I really don't understand it myself. It was some kind of instinctive thoughts, something that we had to do. I believe that Bambalata and myself were chosen. Bambalata was somehow able to travel forward in time to get you. It's thoughts in our minds that has guided us, we don't know how."

Annabell gave up thinking about it. She just accepted the facts of how it was possible for her to time travel 145 million years into the past were not known but she really wanted to know the reason why.

"What is it that you want me to do, giant animal?" asked Annabell rubbing her eyes.

"Please don't be afraid, but I want you to sit on my back."

He lowered his head and lifted her onto it, and then on to his long neck. She slid down his neck like it was a slide that you would find in a children's playground.

Annabell gave out a cry of joy as she slid down onto his back. She no longer felt any fear and asked the animal what his name was.

"My name is Pete," replied the giant animal.

"Pete? But that's a human name, how on earth did you get to be called Pete? Nobody would call a dinosaur that, for Pete's sake," Annabell laughed. "Oh, I'm sorry, that's not funny, but that's what English people say. I think it means like when someone is surprised at the answer to a question but I'm not sure." Annabell couldn't help laughing at her own joke again. "I'm sorry," she said, not very sincerely.

"I thought that you would be called *Bronto* or something like that?"

Pete was really happy to see Annabell laughing, although he didn't understand the joke himself.

Pete told Annabell to hold on tightly and he started walking. He walked very slowly, she could see that he was very weak. All that she could hear was THUMP! - THUMP! -THUMP! as his giant feet were hitting the ground.

Pete walked for about fifteen minutes, until he came to a valley near a river. Pete lowered his head to show Annabell what was in the valley. Annabell was shocked at what she saw.

In the valley were dinosaur bones, hundreds of them. It was obvious that a lot of dinosaurs had died here. It was like what elephants do when they all go to the same place to die. This was a dinosaur graveyard, it seemed to go on and on. Annabell closed her eyes. She was saddened by the sight of this and just wanted to be out of this terrible, horrible place.

Pete walked on still going very slowly it felt like every step was a huge effort for him. Eventually he stopped between two massive rocks. Pete walked between them. There was a hidden cave, if you didn't know it was there you would never find it.

The cave descended into the mountain. It was really dark inside the cave. Annabell was a bit frightened, she didn't like the dark.

She screamed, "PETE! - PETE ! I'm frightened, there had better not be any *spiders* in here."

"Don't worry Annabell there are no spiders in here," Pete assured her.

"But how do you know? I can't see a thing. I don't know how you know where you're going." Annabell gripped Pete's neck even more tightly.

They turned a corner of a narrow passage, Pete's body was scraping the sides of the walls, it was a wonder that he didn't get stuck. Then in front of them Annabell could see a golden light, Pete headed towards the light. It led into a big cavern, all the walls and ceiling were pure *gold* and the floor was like sand but it wasn't sand, it was gold dust!

"We're here now," said Pete. "This is the place." He was becoming weaker and weaker. He staggered over to a hole in the cave wall.

"What's in there?" asked Annabell

"It's my family," said Pete. With those words a tear drop rolled down from his eye, down his cheek and dropped onto the golden floor with a splash.

Annabell looked inside the hole. "But they're just eggs," said Annabell. "And they're big, in fact, huge! I've never seen such big eggs. WOW!" she said loudly.

"These are my children to be, Annabell," said Pete proudly.

"Really!" said Annabell. "How wonderful! How many children, I mean, eggs have you got Pete?"

"Six," he replied.

Pete guided her over to another hole in the wall, inside were another thirty eggs. Pete gave another sigh and a sniff. He was trying so hard to hold back the tears. There was yet another hole which contained another ten eggs.

"This is the reason why you have been brought here, Annabell. I want you to take my family and all the other eggs from all different families forward into your time. We were here long before humans. We have a right to live on the Earth. It's not our fault that there was a disaster here in our time. It's the will of something beyond our comprehension that wants us to survive on Earth into the future. Annabell, you have been brought here so that you can take the eggs back to your time and hatch them out and look after our young."

Annabell looked puzzled. "But how can I do that? Don't you have to sit on the eggs to hatch them out like chickens do? I can't sit on the eggs! They're too big! I'm only little. How can I possibly be able to hatch out the eggs?" Annabell shook her head, as if to say that she wouldn't be able to do that.

"No, Annabell." Pete gave what looked like a grin of some kind. "Don't be silly, you don't have to sit on the eggs. you have the powers to be able to hatch out the eggs."

"But how do you know this? Who told you this? Why me?"

Pete told Annabell a strange story of how a magic object was found millions of years ago. He told her that the Earth started to cool down, instead of it being tropical and hot, which was ideal for dinosaurs. It turned very cold. Dinosaurs lay their eggs in the ground and they hatch out by themselves, but it became too cold on Earth for the eggs to hatch out. No baby dinosaurs were born for over twenty years, dinosaurs were aging and dying. Then one day, a dinosaur laid her eggs as she had done every year for the past twenty years without success, but this time they hatched out - nine babies were born, the first in twenty years. She had laid her eggs on a mysterious object, this object seemed to have had magic powers. But it only had powers for her. She had the power to give life. Once the eggs were touched by the magic object they hatched out. It was told that she picked up the object, and something happened to her. This was only a story though, Annabell, and there was no way of knowing if the story was true until you were born. Now I believe it was true, in fact, I know that it was true."

Annabell was a bit confused by Pete's story.

"What has the story got to do with me?" asked Annabell. "How can I hatch out the eggs? I'm not a dinosaur!"

"I forgot to tell you something, Annabell. The dinosaur that saved us had a red birthmark! I believe that you now have that magic object around your neck, only the one born red has the power. It's you Annabell that's why you were sent for. When you activated the magic object. Bambalata was able to pick up the signals that the object started relaying. I didn't know Bambalata - he's from a different time. His task was to bring you here."

"But what time is Bambalata from?" asked Annabell She was getting very confused.

"It's 70 million years from now, Annabell."

"But how can Bambalata know to pick me up from his time and take me to your time if it's 80 million years apart?" asked Annabell

"I don't know," said Pete. "But he did, because you're here."

Pete told Annabell that the object could be a holy object but he didn't really know much about it. He just knew the story so it had to be a pretty special object.

Annabell thought for several moments about what Pete was telling her. "But if I take your kind back to my time, people will be frightened of you. You're so big, where would you go?"

Pete thought about this question. He knew that it was a good question.

"We're harmless animals, Annabell. We would not harm humans. Alright, we are big but don't you have big animals on the ground amongst you already?"

Annabell thought for a moment, "Elephants are big and the water whales are really big." Pete was right. "YES," she said. "I will do it for you Pete. I will take the eggs and hatch them out, don't you worry about that."

Pete thanked Annabell. "I haven't got much time left, I grow very weak. Soon I will die and join my ancestors."

Annabell started to cry. "I don't want you to die Pete." She cried and cried. Pete story was very sad. She eventually cried herself to sleep still sitting on Pete's back.

She slept all night, when she finally woke up, she found herself in the nest that Bambalata had made for her. Inside the nest were forty-six eggs- plus ten sacks of gold! This would be too much of a weight for Bambalata to carry, but as if by a miracle they were reduced in size and weight for the journey. They would go back to their normal size when Annabell touched them with the magic object.

Pete was lying on the ground next to the nest. He'd worked all through the night getting things prepared. He'd put Annabell into the nest when she was asleep. He was now so weak that he was unable to get up on to his feet.

The mountain was getting very angry, explosions were happening all over it and the toxic smoke was making it hard to breathe. The ground under Annabell's feet was shaking violently. She knew that she would have to leave this mountain and this time on Earth very soon.

Annabell got out of the nest and clutched Pete's head, lovingly. She no longer had any fear for dinosaurs, she knew that they were very gentle and loving animals.

She stroked Pete's head and promised him that she would look after the eggs. Pete whispered to her, now barely able to talk, he told her that the gold would help to look after the new babies when they were born. He seemed to know that human kind regard this metal as valuable.

Annabell lay by the side of Pete for over an hour, comforting him and she was sobbing all the time.

The mountain was becoming more and more ferocious. Bambalata flew down and told Annabell to get inside the nest quickly.

Annabell got up from the ground, she hadn't realised that Pete had died! Her dress was soaking wet from the tears from Pete's eyes.

The mountain roared with fury. Tears were rolling freely down Annabell's red cheeks as she tried to get back into the nest.

"COME ON !" shouted Bambalata. We've got to go now, there's no time to lose, the mountain is going to explode. "Annabell, hurry!"

Annabell clambered into the nest as fast as she could. She took a last look at Pete who was lying peacefully on the ground.

Bambalata tied the nest to his legs - he then tied the top of the nest so that Annabell was secure. There wasn't a moment to lose, every second counted.

Chapter Five
Annabell's Return

Bambalata flapped his wings but couldn't lift off the ground, the extra weight of the eggs and gold were holding him back. There were also lots of conifers which made it difficult for him to take off.

He flapped his wings as fast as he could. He flapped, and flapped, eventually he just managed to lift off the ground with Annabell safely secured inside the nest. Annabell could feel the nest being touched by the top of the trees as they rose from the ground. There wasn't a moment to lose. Annabell could see through a gap in the nest.

The Earth shuddered with a huge earthquake. A huge explosion rocked the mountain to its foundations. Jets of steam shot up high into the sky, followed by thick dense smoke that would instantly kill anything that breathed it!

Bambalata flew away from the mountain as fast as he could. When they were a few miles out at sea, there was an almighty explosion. The loudest noise that Annabell had ever heard. It felt like the Earth was breaking in half. A few moments later there was another huge roar - the ocean shook violently. The mountain that Annabell had just come from exploded, it was like it had been hit by a massive bomb! The mountain was blown to pieces. Debris came falling from the sky and was hitting the water like scatter bombs.

The ocean rose to an alarming height. Huge gaps opened up in the ocean. The sea water cascaded down them like a massive waterfall. It seemed like the whole ocean was being swallowed up inside the Earth.

Annabell screamed, "BAMBALATA YOU MUST GO FASTER!"

Bambalata shouted back, "Don't you think I know that, Annabell?"

He flapped his wings at great speed but his fastest speed was only 30 mph. Bits of the debris from the mountain were flashing by them, like missiles! It was a miracle that they didn't get hit. Eventually they were safe and out of range. Everything seemed different. It seemed to get incredibly cold for a while then it warmed up.

Bambalata flew all through the night, his giant wings enabled him to glide great distances but he was also flying rapidly forward in time - like a time machine.

Meanwhile back at Mr Jacobs' farm concern for Annabell was mounting.

Newspaper, radio and television people from all over the world were gathering.

The story of missing Annabell was now worldwide news because a man named Thomas King just happened to be out filming the countryside wild life, near to Farmer Jacobs' farm when he witnessed this strange phenomenon of a young red girl *dangling* in mid - air. He took a film of it - it showed the girl was flying unaided and in a strange position, and the girl was definitely Annabell.

Experts had studied the film and they were all unanimous that the film was genuine. The incredible film was being relayed around the world.

The man that the police had told to "clear off!" earlier, was re interviewed, they now knew that he was telling the truth and he was given an apology.

Mr Jacobs and Mrs Jacobs were absolutely frantic with worry and feared that they would never see their daughter ever again.

People from all over the world were asked to look out for any sightings of the flying red girl! A report had come through that a possible sighting had been made hundreds of miles out at sea.

The United States of America air force was put on alert. Several jet fighters were scrambled and sent to the last sighting of the flying red girl, but they later returned and reported seeing nothing.

Bambalata flew all through the night. It was nearly daybreak when he reached Annabell's home. It was not known how it was possible for Bambalata to travel through time or how he found his way back to the exact time that Annabell lived in.

There was nobody about and it was still quite dark. He landed very quietly near the farm house.

Annabell was still fast asleep, she was warm and comfortable in her nest and didn't know that she was home. Bambalata released the nest and quickly flew off before it got too light. Bambalata would never be seen again.

Farmer Jacobs and Mrs Jacobs were unaware that their daughter was home. It wasn't until 8:00am that morning when the police knocked on their door telling them that there was a strange object not far from the farmhouse. The police told them that it looked like a giant bird's nest! Farmer Jacobs ran out of the house as fast as he could. Mrs Jacobs was right behind him.

The police led them to the object. "What is it, Bill?" asked Mrs Jacobs.

"I don't know dear," he replied, "I've never seen anything like it. What on God's Earth could it be? It does look like a giant bird's nest."

Farmer Jacobs went over to it, escorted by the police. By this time the news media were back at the farm in force. They had been gathering at the same time every day just after 8:00 am.

The Chief of police carefully untied the binding that connected the top of the nest. He pulled off the top to reveal Annabell. Mr. Jacobs yelled,

"IT'S MY DAUGHTER! - IT'S ANNABELL! Is she alright, she's not moving?"

Lots of flash cameras were set off at the same time. The news people jostled forward to try and get a better look. The police had to form a circle around the nest to keep them away.

Farmer Jacobs carefully prodded his daughter, he could see that she was fast asleep. "Pinky, wake up… Pinky wake up." Slowly Annabell opened her eyes. At first she wasn't sure where she was. The lights from the cameras were flashing in her eyes. She rubbed her eyes and suddenly recognised who it was who was talking to her. "DADDY! - DADDY! AND MUMMY! Oh, I've missed you so much," said Annabell.

"Where have you been, daughter?" asked Farmer Jacobs. "Me and Mummy have been so worried about you, are you hurt?"

"No daddy, I've been to the mountain to see Pete. Bambalata took me there." Tears came into Annabell's eyes. " He died, daddy, but I've brought his family back and other families as well."

"What are you talking about darling? What family? Who's Pete, and Bambalata?"

"I've got Pete's family here in the nest." Annabell lifted up one of the eggs from the nest. "Look!" she said. "This is his child!"

Annabell had in her hand what looked like a duck egg. It was a strange colour though. It was a bright white covered with blue specks.

Farmer Jacobs was flabbergasted. He couldn't believe what his daughter was saying.

"What on Earth have you got there, Pinky?"

The news people flashed their cameras at the strange egg. There were gasps from the people. News had quickly filtered out that Annabell had been found. More and more media people and ordinary local people were amassing at the farm. Extra police had to be rushed in. Police sirens could be heard in the distance. coming from everywhere.

"What is that egg, Annabell?" asked the Chief police officer, Frank Murgett.

"It's a dinosaur egg, silly!"

"Dinosaur?" The police officer covered his mouth trying not to laugh, but he couldn't help laughing and everybody else started to laugh. Annabell had become the subject of some amusement.

"Why are you laughing at me?" she said, angrily. "It's true! And I've got forty-five more and I've got lots of gold that Pete gave me to look after the babies when they're born." Annabell put her hand into one of the small sacks of gold and grabbed a handful and threw it onto the ground for everybody to see. "There!" she said. "I told you, so don't laugh at me please. I might be a little girl but I'm not stupid."

The gold was examined by an expert jeweller who just happened to be there. " My!" he said "It is gold, and it's the most beautiful gold that I've ever seen, it's so pure, it's perfect! Where did you get this from, child?"

"I got it from the mountain. Pete gave it to me. There was a cave and it was made out of gold, even the floor!"

"What mountain?" asked the jeweller. "There has never ever been gold found like this before, just look at the colour of it, look how it shines! It's worth a fortune."

"The mountain is gone! It blew up!" said Annabell, in a sad voice.

"But where was the mountain?" asked the jeweller. He had a look of gold fever in his eyes! It was the look that people get when they think that they can get or make lots of easy money.

"It's gone! I told you, so there's no point in looking for it - it blew up! Exploded! It went bang! It's gone forever. It was a volcano that existed 145 million years ago.

Some news person shouted out, "How do you know that?"

"Because I do - I was there - I saw it."

"How can you see something that happened 145 million years ago?" somebody shouted out. "That's ridiculous!"

"I don't know, but I did," said Annabell sternly. "Bambalata took me to the mountain. He was able to time travel. He took me to see Pete. He needed my help. He needed me to save his kind and I will. I promised that I would, and I'm going to." Annabell spoke very sternly. She was committed to her promise to Pete.

"Who's Pete?... Who's Bambalata?" asked the *NEW TALK TIMES* correspondent, Ted Boxley.

"Pete is...or should I say, was, a dinosaur! Who lived on the mountain with lots of other dinosaurs but they're all dead now. I saw all their bones in the valley. And Bambalata is some kind of bird thing."

"So a bird took you back 145 million years in time to see a dinosaur?" said Ted. "I'll tell you what girl - I'll give you ten thousand dollars for your story."

"I'll give you twenty thousand," said somebody else.

"Fifty thousand!" said Ted.

A bidding war had started for Annabell's story from the media. It quickly got out of control and reached a million dollars!

"I DON'T WANT YOUR MONEY!" Annabell shouted out. "I've got all the money that I need, Pete gave it to me."

All the crowd wanted to know what the eggs really were.

"We don't believe that the eggs are dinosaurs," somebody shouted. "How can they be? Dinosaurs died out millions of years ago, and birds didn't exist, everybody knows that, you're making it all up."

Mr Jacobs butted in. "Please don't talk to my daughter like that, if you don't mind."

Annabell was beginning to get angry. "None of you understand, why don't you all just go away and leave me alone," she yelled.

"It's all been a hoax, we've be taken for mugs," shouted one of the press people.

"What a ridiculous story, giant birds! Dinosaurs! Whatever next?" somebody shouted.

Annabell stood up in the nest and shouted at all the people at the top of her voice,

"I HAVE SOMETHING VERY IMPORTANT TO SHOW YOU BUT FIRST I WILL TELL YOU MY STORY AND YOU CAN ALL HAVE IT - FREE OF CHARGE!!!"

Annabell started telling about the fantastic adventure that she'd had. Everybody stood there and listened. It was so quiet that you could hear a pin drop! When Annabell had finished, to her surprise, everybody started to laugh!

Annabell was very upset and started to cry. Farmer Jacobs and Mrs Jacobs put their arms around their daughter to comfort her.

"Never mind Pinky, darling," said Mr Jacobs. "It's a lovely story, but it's a bit hard to believe. Dinosaurs haven't been living on the Earth for millions of years, there's only fossil bones left now!"

" But it's true daddy, I can prove it."

With those words *prove it* the news people stopped laughing and they started to take notice.

"How can you prove it?" shouted a man from the British *BCC* Television. A rather arrogant looking man with a scruffy unkempt beard and a dirty raincoat. His name was Cecil Falkner.

Annabell didn't like this man, he talked funny as well! He wasn't speaking in an American accent. He sounded very pompous.

"Because," … Annabell paused and bided her time with the explanation. "…Because I can hatch out the egg!" she said proudly.

"Hatch out the egg?" Cecil shouted back somewhat insultingly. "What, you a chicken or something?" With those words he started dancing around flapping his arms like a chicken and making chicken noises.

Everybody started to laugh at this man's joke.

Annabell had enough of these rude people and lifted the egg that was in her hand. She lifted it high in the air so that everybody could see it. The egg wasn't that big for such a big creature, and it wasn't heavy.

"That's too small to be a dinosaur egg," somebody shouted out. "A brachiosaurus egg is nearly a foot long. You've got a goose egg."

The crowd laughed again, they were all having fun with Annabell's story.

Annabell touched the egg with her magic necklace piece that her dad had found. She remembered what Pete had told her about the powers of the object. The egg started to grow, until it was what that man had said, a foot long.

Mr Jacobs was very concerned when he saw the necklace and the object attached to it.

"Daughter, where did you get that from? I thought that I had got rid of it forever."

Annabell didn't answer, she knew that she'd been a naughty girl not telling her mummy and daddy that she had it, but she knew that she had to have it.

The egg started to glow, it got brighter and brighter, so too were Annabell's eyes! This was always a sign that her powers were working.

She didn't know if it would work but Pete said it would, if it didn't, her trip would have been a waste of time but she was very confident that it would work.

Everybody stood there in silence. Nothing happened for a while, but the egg was still glowing.

Those horrible people once again started to jeer and laugh at her. Then all of a sudden the egg started to crack. Slowly the cracks got bigger and bigger. Then a small hole appeared and out of the egg popped a little head! Slowly something crawled out of the shell and rested into Annabell's hand.

Everybody was flabbergasted at what they had just seen. Annabell said in a high-pitched voice of excitement, " I TOLD YOU SO!"

Everybody rushed forward to get a photograph of the baby creature.

"It's a baby alligator." said one of the newsmen.

"No, I think that it's a crocodile, I've seen baby crocodiles before. I'm certain that's what it is," shouted the horrible man from the *BCC,* Cecil.

A man at the back of the crowd shouted , "Everybody please get out of the way, quickly! Let me through. I must look at this creature. I'm a Paleontologist and work for the natural history museum, I know about these things. My name is Professor Barnett. Please let me through." The professor made his way through the crowd.

He studied the baby creature for several minutes using his magnifying glass. He carefully examined the creature and produced a book from his coat pocket that had the history and descriptions of all dinosaurs that had lived on the Earth. He shook his head. Then he mumbled something and yelled out uncontrollably. "MY GOD! HOW CAN THIS POSSIBLY BE? IT'S...IT'S ... IT'S... A... BABY BRACHIOSAURUS!"

The professor fainted and fell to the floor. The excitement of the discovery was too much for him. Never in his wildest dreams did he ever think that he would ever see a living dinosaur.

The professor was brought round with smelling salts. He started mumbling something.

"E rr...er r...um, what shall I do?... um- what shall I do?" He was squeezing his lips with his finger and thumb trying to think of what to do. "Yes, er...um. We must inform the President at once... yes at once. He has to know about this. This is a very...very...very... serious situation indeed."

The police chief asked why it was so serious, "It's only a baby." He said smugly, "Why would the President want to know about a baby crocodile?"

"Didn't you hear me sir?" said the Professor. "This is not a baby crocodile. Do you know what a Brachiosaurus is, man? It's one of the biggest dinosaurs ever to walk this Earth. This *baby* as you call it will grow to be between maybe thirty and seventy tonnes in weight and will be nearly one hundred feet long, and forty feet high, sir! That's why the President needs to know. It been extinct for millions of years."

"Oh!" said the police chief. "I see what you mean."

The police chief quickly removed all the people away from the farm, road blocks were set up all around it. Absolutely nobody would be allowed anywhere near the farm if they didn't have the authority to do so.

Government officials were called in. Annabell was told by one of them - a man wearing dark glasses and neatly dressed in a suit, that she would have to hand over the baby creature.

Annabell said, "Please don't hurt baby Pete, I promised his dad that I would take care of him." She cuddled the baby dinosaur in her arms like it was a kitten and wouldn't let it go.

The government agents gave their word that no harm would come to the baby dinosaur.

A blue armoured van pulled up with steel bars on the windows. Two men got out and put on protective clothing and told Annabell to hand over the creature.

Annabell didn't want to but she knew that she had no choice, she gave the baby a kiss and handed him over very reluctantly. One of the agents who was wearing thick gloves took it from her.

"YOU'D BETTER NOT HURT HIM," Annabell shouted out to him.

He placed baby Pete in a container and put him into the van. All the eggs were gathered up and also placed in the van. Shortly afterwards another van pulled up - this was an armoured van. This was sent to pick up the gold.

The two vans left the farm together. They were escorted by five police cars in front and five police cars at the back. Two helicopters flew overhead. All the police cars had their lights flashing and their sirens blaring out.

A doctor was called to examine Annabell, she was found to be in perfect health.

She was told that she must make a full statement to the government agents about her adventures when she was ready.

The news of the baby dinosaur and the eggs and the gold - soon travelled around the world. This was a big story for the Earth. Everybody was interested to know exactly what Annabell had been up to. Her story was so incredible - but there was evidence in the form of a baby dinosaur. Where had Annabell got this from? And all the eggs? And she had massive amount of gold. Nobody really believed her story but the facts were there for all to see.

Annabell didn't know it but she was never ever in any danger when she wore the necklace with the object- she became immortal, absolutely nothing could harm her.

Annabell already had the power herself to time-travel but she wasn't yet aware of it. She would learn of this power at a later date.

⸺⋘◇⋙⸺

Chapter Six

Questioning by Government Agents

A government agent later picked Annabell up along with Mr and Mrs Jacobs and took them to a secure government building for questioning.

First question to Annabell was asked by agent Marc Primo. He was a big man. He had a body like a heavyweight boxer. Some people nicknamed him *ROCKY* after the old classic film made over two hundred years ago.

Also in the room was a female agent called Serena Plant. Serena was of mixed race, twenty eight years old and a rather beautiful woman. Annabell took a liking to her straight away but it was probably because she gave her a sweet and it was one of Annabell's favourites. (cough candy).

"Umm," muttered Marc, "I believe your name is Annabell Jacobs and you live at Cherry Tree Farm with your mummy and daddy, and you're eight years old. Is that correct?"

Marc knew full well who she was but he had to be formal. Although Marc was a big man he had a quiet voice and was a gentle, friendly man.

"Yes sir," said Annabell politely. "But my daddy calls me just *Pinky!* But that's a nickname. Mummy calls me Annabell though because she doesn't like the name Pinky, she's always telling my daddy off about it. But I don't mind my daddy calling me that. He calls me that because of the colour of my skin."

"I guessed that Annabell," said Marc. "Is it alright if I call you Pinky?"

Annabell looked at Marc with a frown on her face. "No! it's not alright. Definitely not all right. Only my daddy can call me that."

"Oh!" said Marc "Ok then, sorry!" He was a bit taken back by Annabell's answer but carried on with the interview.

"You can call me Marc and I'm sure Miss Plant would rather you call her Serena or Rena as we call her here at the office." Serena nodded in approval.

"Umm... Annabell," Marc paused, "where did you get the eggs from?"

"From Pete, on his mountain," said Annabell, screwing up her little nose.

"Who's Pete?" asked Serena.

"He's a dinosaur, but he died, they all died on the mountain."

"Pete is a strange name for a dinosaur Annabell, are you sure that you're not making this up?"

"No! I'm most certainly not," said Annabell rather angrily. She couldn't understand why people didn't believe her.

"Where was the mountain Annabell ? Is it near here?" asked Marc

"Oh, I don't know sir. Oh, I mean, Marc. Bambalata took me there. I thought that it was a long way because Bambalata flew all night but I didn't know that we were travelling back in time - so it's impossible to know where it was because we must have been moving back in years rather than distance."

"Who's Bambalata?" asked Marc.

"He's a giant bird thing!" replied Annabell.

"Giant bird? What sort of bird would that be Annabell?" asked Serena. "The biggest bird on the Earth I think is an ostrich, and it can't fly. Eagles are pretty big but I don't think they'll be able to lift you off the ground. So what bird was it, Annabell?"

"I don't know what bird he was. He wouldn't tell me. He said that I wouldn't understand."

"What did the bird look like?" asked Serena.

Annabell thought for a moment. "Er…umm, it had - umm, a funny sort of thing on top of its head, like… umm, a witch's hat. And…um, it had really long wings, about well, as big as me! Even bigger! And that's each wing. He had a small body though with little legs, with big claws as feet. Even with his big wings Bambalata found it hard to take off - but when he was in the air he found it easy to fly, most of the time he just glided."

Marc wrote in his note book the description of the bird that Annabell was telling him. He picked up the telephone and talked to somebody, you could hear him describing the bird. A short while later Marc said to the person on the other end of the line. "Really! You've got to be joking," and then he put the phone down.

"Hmm…Annabell…The 'bird' that you're describing is not a bird, it's a flying reptile called a pteranodon or something like that. Which has been extinct for a least 80 million years," said Marc in a higher than usual voice.

"Ah, well," said Annabell. "There you go then, I thought that he was a bird. I knew that he came from 80 million years ago, because Pete told me. But at least that proves that what I've been telling you is all true. I knew that there was something odd about him, he was so ugly, I told him that to his face but I suppose he would look ugly if he was over 80 million years old, and was a reptile," laughed Annabell.

"Umm, oh, dear," muttered Marc. "Oh, dear Annabell, your story can't be true because according to the scientist or paleontologist or whatever you call them people, your baby dinosaur, Annabell, is a Brachiosaurus which comes from a time 145 million years ago. So how can a creature born around 70 million years before the other creature take you to see the other creature?" asked Marc, shaking his head.

"That's easy," said Annabell. "Bambalata picked up the signal from my necklace and travelled forward in time to find me. He had been sent to do the task and then he was guided back past his time into Pete's time, so that I could pick up the eggs before they were destroyed. And then he brought me back to my time. I assume he's now back in his time."

Marc laughed. "Well I must say Annabell you have a fantastic imagination. Wow! Oh, well, let's move on," said Marc. "Have you any questions, Serena?"

"Yes I have, could you tell me something Annabell, how did you know his name was Bambalata? And the dinosaur's name was Pete?" Serena really thought that this would stump her.

"Because they told me their names," said Annabell shrugging her shoulder as if to say 'what a stupid question to ask'.

But Marc and Serena were puzzled by her answer.

"So… umm, you can speak to animals, can you?" asked agent Marc with a grin on his face. Marc looked over to Serena and shrugged his shoulders as if to say 'this is getting ridiculous'.

"Yes sir, I can speak to animals, and birds, and in fact, any living thing on this Earth," said Annabell, cockily.

Agent Primo and agent Plant both looked at each other and were shocked by Annabell's answer but they thought that it was a joke.

"Well that's rather a clever thing to do. I've never heard of anybody who could speak to animals. How do you do that Annabell? If you don't mind me asking," said Marc.

"Because..." Annabell looked Marc straight into his eyes. "...Because, I've got magic powers, sir. That's how."

"Ah, well that would explain it then," joked Marc. "Did you hear that, Serena? Annabell has got magic powers: isn't that fantastic?" Marc and Serena both laughed out loud.

Annabell didn't care though, she was used to people laughing at her - so she just blew a raspberry at them. (That means to make a rude noise by blowing through her tongue).

"I don't care if you laugh at me," she said. "But I have got magic powers, it's my magic necklace piece that daddy found in his field. It gives me powers."

"Really? Can I see your magic necklace, Annabell," asked Marc.

The object was glowing brightly on Annabell's gold necklace and did look rather strange and intriguing.

Annabell took it off her neck and handed it over to Marc.

Instantly it stopped glowing and turned a drab grey colour.

"It doesn't look much, Annabell, will it have magic powers for me?" asked Marc twiddling the object around in his fingers.

"No sir, only me, I was chosen, I'm the chosen one. Pete told me that."

"The chosen one, Annabell? Who chose you?"

"I don't know," said Annabell, "but that's what I was told."

Marc had an idea that he believed would prove that what Annabell was saying was nonsense.

"Er... umm, Annabell ...you know, umm- that you said that you could talk to animals."

"Yeah," said Annabell.

"If I brought in my pet hamster do you think that you'll be able to talk to him?"

"Yes sir, I definitely would," said Annabell confidently.

Agent Primo nodded his head and sighed. "Ok, then, well see." He picked up the phone and asked for his pet hamster to be brought from his home to the office.

Thirty minutes later the animal was brought into the room in his cage and placed onto the table.

"I'll ask you again, Annabell. You can change your mind if you want to. Can you talk to this hamster and understand what it says, because I'm going to ask you a series of questions that only I will know? Do you understand that ?"

"Yes sir," said Annabell. "But I will need my necklace back, otherwise I won't be able to do it."

Agent Primo handed Annabell back her necklace. She put it around her neck. Instantly it started to glow with all the colours of the rainbow.

"Are you ready, Annabell?" Marc looked over to Serena with a look that suggested that this was going to be fun.

"Yes sir, I'm ready," said Annabell, admiring the hamster.

"Will you ask Fred, my hamster, what time did I give him his food this morning?"

Annabell asked the hamster the question in English. The hamster just gave out a few squeaking noises.

"Yeah, got it," said Annabell smiling, something had amused her.

"George? Not Fred! says that you gave her breakfast at 8:17am and you keep her in your bedroom and she says that she likes you but you snore and keep her awake!"

Agent Primo was shocked and shook his head in disbelief. "What? We didn't know that she was a girl! And you're quite right his - her? name is George. I was trying to trick you. And I did give him, oh, I mean her - her breakfast as you say at about 8:15 give or take a few minutes. Everything that you told me so far has been correct, Annabell, that's brilliant!"

But Marc thought that Annabell may have had a lucky guess at the hamster's name and the time that he had fed the hamster but knew that it was hardy unlikely.

"Can you ask her how old she is because I know for sure her exact birth date."

Annabell asked the hamster some questions. A few squeaks later,

"Yeah, got it," said Annabell. "George says that she's one year two months and twenty days old! And that your wife's name is Melody and you've been married for eight years and have two children named Maxine and Doreen and she says that you should stop smoking because it's bad for your health and the smoke is getting in her eyes! And can you please change her name because she doesn't like being called a boy's name?" Then Annabell laughed out loud, she knew that Marc would have to believe her now.

Annabell was right. Agent Marc Primo had no doubts now that Annabell did have powers and that she could talk to animals. He turned to agent Serena Plant and gave her a look of astonishment and shrugged his shoulders to suggest that he really didn't know what was happening here. Serena did likewise, she was flabbergasted, she'd never seen anything like it.

But there were still a few more questions that needed answers. Serena couldn't wait to ask Annabell a question that everybody wanted to know.

Serena pulled open a drawer that was in the desk and pulled out the film that was taken of her apparently *flying*. She put it into a playing machine and asked Annabell to watch it.

Annabell sat there and watched it, she was fascinated by the film. She knew exactly what was happening. She was being carried by Bambalata but only she could see him. So it appeared to everyone else that she was flying - it looked so funny to her. Annabell was laughing so much that she nearly fell out of the chair that she was sitting in.

"Alright, Annabell. I give in, How did you do that? Can you really fly?" asked Serena.

"Oh, dear!" said Annabell still laughing. "No, of course I can't fly, it was Bambalata. He had hold of me with his claws but obviously only I can see him. I know that you won't believe me."

"But I do," said Serena. "Oh, yes, I do - everything that you have told us has been true, you've proved it to us. I have absolutely no reason to doubt you now, Annabell. What a fantastic and brave little girl you are. It must have been wonderful to go back 145 million years."

"It was and it wasn't, ma'am. It was so sad. I saw what happened to the mountain and the dinosaurs. It felt like it was the end of the world - it was for the dinosaurs on that mountain. But something good has come out of it. I've hopefully saved some of them. That's if the government will allow them to live."

Marc looked over at Annabell and asked her in a serious but sincere voice.

"What do you want us to do, Annabell?"

"Marc… sir. I promised Pete before he died that I would hatch out all the eggs and let the dinosaurs live back on the Earth, after all, as he told me. They were here before us. Pete gave me the gold so that they would be looked after."

Marc asked the Jacobs family to excuse him while he left the room for a while. He told them that he had a very important call to make. He had to phone the President of the United States of America. He knew that this was a very serious situation.

"Annabell my dear," said Marc, "you've set us a bit of a problem, young lady. I really don't know what the President is going to say. Oh, dear. What's he going to make of this, I wonder? I won't be long." Marc was wiping away sweat from his brow with his hand as he talked to Annabell. "I'm dreading this call, Annabell. I'll try my best, that's all that I can say." Marc left the room.

He was gone for over an hour! The conversation had obviously been difficult. Annabell in that time had eaten all of Serena's sweets!

Marc at last came back into the room.

"I've had a word with the President, Annabell. My, you've caused us a lot of hard thinking, everybody in the world wants to talk to you - you've become very famous, young lady. All that I can say at this time is that there's going to be a meeting in the morning with the United Nations to discuss what is to be done. Not one Nation has the right to decide such a serious issue as this. Dinosaurs living back amongst people. Who would have thought it? The scientists, Annabell, will have to decide whether it's safe for these giant creatures to be able to live again. I must warn you though if the answer is no, the baby dinosaur that you hatched out will have to be put down I'm afraid. I'm very sorry but we would have no choice."

"NO!- NO! You mustn't do that," said Annabell sternly. "I gave my word to Pete."

"I'm sorry, Annabell, but it's not up to me, if I had my way, I'd love to see dinosaurs back living on the Earth with us, it would be a fantastic sight."

Annabell was very concerned as to what had happened to baby Pete since she was forced to hand him over.

"What have you done with baby Pete? You'd better not have harmed him, these creatures are gentle, they wont harm anybody, I'm telling you it's a fact," pleaded Annabell

"Don't worry, don't upset yourself. Baby Pete is being well cared for. I know that for certain Annabell," said Marc sincerely. "I'm sorry but I've been ordered by the President that I must take the magic object off you."

"But it won't work for anybody else," yelled Annabell. "Nobody can hatch out the eggs, *only me,*" she moaned.

"We know that, please remove it from your neck, I have to have it, Annabell, it's my orders and I have to follow orders, especially from the President. I have no choice."

Marc moved towards Annabell to remove the necklace.

"No! I don't want you to have it. If you don't give it to me back, I won't be able to keep my promise that I gave to Pete. I'm not going to give it to you."

Annabell got up from the chair and ran to the door trying to get out of the room but Serena quickly blocked her path.

"Sorry Annabell," said Serena. "But if you don't give it to me, I'll have to remove it forcibly and I really don't want to do that."

Serena grabbed hold of Annabell. "Come on Annabell, be a good girl please. Take off the necklace.

Mr Jacobs interrupted. "Hand it over daughter, don't cause a fuss. It's got to be sorted by the experts. Come on darling, give it to Serena, there's a good girl."

Annabell reluctantly handed her necklace over to Serena. Who then handed it to Marc.

"Thank you Annabell," said Marc. "I'll do my best to get it back to you, I promise."

The magic object instantly changed back to its normal drab grey colour. Annabell's eyes weren't so sparkly now either.

Marc advised Mr and Mrs Jacobs that it would be best if they remained in the care of the government because Annabell had created a massive story around the world.

Hundreds of the world's press had gathered at Mr Jacobs' farm, everybody wanted her story. Marc told them that they wouldn't get any peace now that the story was public.

Mr Jacobs reluctantly agreed. They were taken during the hours of darkness to a secret location where hopefully nobody would be able to find them.

They were taken to The White House, the home of the President of the United States of America.

Annabell was so thrilled she couldn't believe that she would be staying at the same place as the President.

Over the next few weeks talks began with every nation taking part. The decision about the dinosaurs affected the whole world, some were for it but others were against it.

The arguments for and against went on and on. All the world's leading scientists were called to give their views. The leading expert in the world of paleontologists a Professor Remi gave a speech to the

United Nations trying to convince them that these creatures were considered to be harmless to humans although very big, in fact, one of the biggest dinosaurs that ever lived but he told them that they were gentle family creatures who lived in harmony, just like our elephants are today. He went on to tell the conference that he couldn't see any reason why these magnificent creatures shouldn't be allowed to re-inhabit the Earth. It would be very exciting to be able to study these animals. Man has been very lucky to be given this chance and he added as a final thought that some people would say that maybe it's "God's Will." and who was he or anybody to deny these fabulous creatures their right to come back to the Earth.

There was a big cheer from the conference room and nearly everybody clapped him and shouts of "Hear!- Hear!" could be heard in agreement.

A vote was taken, every Nation would have a vote.

Several hours passed while the votes were being counted.

The President of the United Nations stood up and started to speak:

" Ladies and Gentlemen a decision has been made by the worlds leaders and it gives me great pleasure to tell you that it's been unanimous. The dinosaurs will be allowed to live back amongst us."

The whole conference hall erupted in a frenzy of excitement. The world's press rushed to get the story out.

Annabell, Mr and Mrs Jacobs were watching the events on the television. Annabell jumped up and screamed at the television in excitement and hugged and kissed her mummy and daddy. "I've done it mummy and daddy - I've done it!" She was so happy that her promise to Pete would be fulfilled.

The next day the President of the United States of America came and talked to Annabell. "You must be a very proud young lady," he said to her sincerely.

Annabell bowed her head, she felt ever so humble and was in awe of being in the company of the most powerful man in the whole world. The President!

"Yes sir," she said, "I thank you with all my heart." And tears came into her eyes, she was remembering Pete. He would be so proud now.

"Don't cry, Annabell," said the President, "come on; hold your head up and be proud." And he gave her a kiss on her cheek. Annabell blushed but nobody could tell because she was already red!

The President took something out of his pocket. "Annabell I've got something to give to you, that's if it's alright with your mummy and daddy?"

He handed her the necklace with the magic object on it. Mr and Mrs Jacobs gave their approval that Annabell could have it back on one condition. "Daughter," said Mrs Jacobs quite sternly. "You can only wear it with my permission. I don't mind you talking to the animals, I know that you're a very special girl. God made you that way and I know that you have powers that nobody can explain but you must be careful with these powers. You must only use them to do good things. Do you agree daughter?"

Annabell nodded. "Yes mummy. Can I wear it now please?" Mrs Jacobs said that she could.

Mrs Jacobs put it around her neck. Instantly it started to change colours.

Annabell's eye's shone brightly too. She was so happy now.

"Wow!" cried out the President. "Would you look at that? It sure is magic of the like that I've never seen before. I wonder what causes it? And where it came from? None of our scientists have any idea what this object is. I wonder why it only works for you,

Annabell? We tried out a test, we placed the object into hundreds of people's hands and it didn't work for any of them!

I must also tell you Annabell that all the gold belongs to you. We've had the value of it estimated by gold dealers and they all agreed that it's the finest and purest gold that they have ever seen. It may come as a bit of a shock to you Annabell, but the gold is valued at - Five Million Dollars! You're a very wealthy little girl."

"That's not the real value," said Annabell. "You valued the gold when it's in small bags. When I touch the bags with the object they will go back to their original size. They will be worth at least ten times that value. None of the gold belongs to me," said Annabell shaking her head. " It's to look after the baby dinosaurs. I promised Pete that I would look after his family and kind. All the money must go to look after them. Nothing for me."

The President gave his word that they would all be looked after.

"I have a special surprise for you Annabell, Please follow me." The President escorted Annabell, and Mr and Mrs Jacobs out of the White House and into a chauffeur driven limousine. It was a huge black stretched car and was driven by a man wearing a cap and dark glasses. Four other men got in the car all wearing dark glasses, they all looked the same.

Annabell was a bit puzzled. "Who are all these people?" she asked.

"Don't worry Annabell, these people are here to guard me."

"But why do you need to be guarded? You're the most powerful man in the world, nobody would harm you."

"The world is volatile Annabell, - just like the Earth. You can never be certain what's going to happen in the future. It would be nice if the world's people lived in peace but they don't, and probably never will. So we must always be careful - one day we may need your help again."

The limousine driver drove off. Annabell didn't know where she was going.

Chapter Seven
Annabell's Surprise

"Where are you taking us, sir?" asked Annabell with a great deal of curiousness. "Wait and see little girl, my you're so inquisitive." The President answered Annabell with a smug look on his face. It was obvious he was hiding a secret. Something that was very special.

They drove up a track which was well off the main road, and they came to two big iron gates. At the gates stood two armed sentry guards. This was government land, there was a sign attached to the gates which told people to *keep out.* Nobody was allowed to go past these gates without special permission from the President himself.

The President handed Annabell and Mr and Mrs Jacobs a badge. They had writing on them which read 'VIP' (very important person). Annabell looked at her badge. It had her name Annabell Jacobs written on it with a photograph of her. But she didn't really need a photo because there wasn't anybody like her in the whole world.

The sentry guards stopped the car and asked to see their identification. Even though they recognised the President he still had to show his pass. Annabell was so proud. She pushed her pass right in front of the sentry's face hitting him on his nose! "Oops," she said, "sorry!"

"It's alright Annabell," said the sentry, "I can see that you're excited. Good morning, President."

"Morning James. Open the gates please."

The guard saluted the President and opened the big gate and they drove down a long dusty road for over five miles. Eventually they came to another gate. Another two sentries stood on guard and the same procedure followed before they opened the gate and let the car through. About ten minutes later the car stopped. The President turned to Mr and Mrs Jacobs, and Annabell, and said quietly, "We're here now - you can get out of the car."

The driver opened the car door for the President, Mr and Mrs Jacobs and Annabell. "Where are we?" shouted Annabell excitedly.

"You'll see. Follow me." The President led them into a large building and was met by a rather frumpy looking woman in a white coat. She had grey hair and was wearing spectacles. She looked like a scientist of some kind.

"Morning President sir," she said politely, "I've been expecting you."

"Morning Professor Hood, how is he?" asked the President, mysteriously.

"Very well sir," came the reply.

"Good! Good!" answered the President, grinning.

"Hello young lady," said Professor Hood, "I know who you are! You're our famous little girl Annabell. It's a pleasure, and I sincerely mean pleasure, to meet you." She held out her hand for Annabell to shake. Which she did.

"Thank you ma'am, and it's a pleasure to meet you too," answered Annabell, "but who are you?"

"You'll see! Please follow me." She led them into a big room and over in the corner in a big cage was baby Pete!

Annabell screamed. "BABY PETE!" She ran over to his cage.

He seemed to recognise her and came to the bars of his cage. Baby Pete had grown quite a lot since Annabell had last seen him. He looked double the size.

"Oh, can I go inside the cage please, I really want to hold my baby?" said Annabell excitedly.

The President turned to Professor Hood and asked her, "Is that alright, Professor?

"Yes, I don't see why not, but we'll have to ask Mr and Mrs Jacobs' permission."

"Yeah, I suppose so," said both of them. "As long as it's safe. I don't want my daughter to get hurt," said Mrs Jacobs anxiously.

"I'll be alright mummy, Baby Pete won't hurt me. He's a gentle creature."

"Ok, go on then, go in," said Mrs Jacobs. "But be careful!"

Professor Hood opened up the cage and Annabell ran in as fast as she could and grabbed hold of baby Pete. She hugged and kissed him. " BABY! - BABY!" she screamed with excitement. " How are you? But baby Pete didn't answer. He couldn't talk yet, he was only a baby and baby dinosaurs can't talk until they're a lot older.

"My you've grown," said Annabell trying to pick the baby dinosaur up but it was a bit too big for her to do that.

Annabell spent over an hour with the baby dinosaur. The President watched in amazement at the incredible sight of a red girl with a baby dinosaur! He had to wipe his eyes several times to see if it was really happening!

It was time for them to go. Annabell kissed the baby and waved him goodbye.

"I have another surprise for you, Annabell," said the President. "Come with me."

He led them outside. Already under construction was, what was going to become the dinosaur's home. The President had given over this land which was vast. It was covered in lush grasses, woodland, and beautiful lakes over to the Dinosaur project.

Although Annabell already had millions of dollars, donations had been coming in from all over the world to support the dinosaurs. A vast amount of money had been collected. The world was united in this project. These creatures when born would be well cared for.

Annabell was overcome with emotion. "Oh my goodness me!" she said. "Just look at this place it's perfect…it's so beautiful here."

"I have one more surprise for you, Annabell," said the President proudly. "Follow me."

He led Annabell to a room inside the main building where there were people making some sort of sign. "Close your eyes, Annabell," said the President.

He held her hand and led her over to the people. "Right my heroic little girl, you can open your eyes now." Annabell slowly opened her eyes and she saw a sign that they were making. "What does the sign say?" asked Annabell. The President said cunningly, "Read it for yourself."

Annabell slowly read out the words.

"ANNABELL'S DINOSAUR WORLD."

"WOW!" she shrieked. "You're going to name their home after me?"

"Yes Annabell ," said the President."I'm so proud of you, we couldn't call it anything else. I want the world to be able to see these magnificent creatures and I want the world never, and I mean **never** to forget who was responsible."

Annabell shook her head in disbelief. She remembered the words that Bambalata had said to her. *"What you will be asked to do, will have a change on the world."*

It was true. Annabell had made a change to the world.

The work to get the Dinosaur World ready took a considerable time to complete.

The day finally arrived for the dinosaur eggs to be hatched out. It was very close to Annabell's birthday. She was born on 9th of March at 4:30pm. It was decided that at precisely 4:30pm on the 9th March the dinosaur eggs will be hatched out by Annabell, which was two days away.

The big day arrived. The most important people from all over the world had been invited to witness the birth of the baby Dinosaurs.

ANNABELL'S DINOSAUR WORLD was finished and it was magnificent. A huge double wire fence had been erected all around the land. All the very latest security systems were in place to safeguard these creatures. Security guards were placed all around the perimeter of the fence. Nobody would ever be able to get in amongst the dinosaurs without permission.

Guided tours would be arranged for people to be able to see these creatures. The President wanted them to be for the people of the world but already demand to see them was huge. The waiting list was already two years long, and rising.

Everything was now ready. Annabell was there with her mummy and daddy right next to the President. The Prime Minister of England, Australia and India stood close by.

At precisely 4:00pm an armoured van pulled up with ten security people who were guarding the contents of the van. They unloaded very carefully each egg onto the ground on a straw bed. All forty-five eggs were now ready for Annabell to hatch out. The time now was 4:29pm+50 seconds. The people attending started a countdown.

"TEN - NINE - EIGHT - SEVEN - SIX - FIVE - FOUR - THREE - TWO - ONE."

A huge roar went up as Annabell touched each egg with her magic object. They all started to glow yellow, cracks started appearing. One by one little heads popped out of the shells. In no time at all forty-five baby dinosaurs were born.

Everybody started singing loudly. "HAPPY BIRTHDAY DEAR DINOSAURS" and they ended with "A HAPPY BIRTHDAY DEAR ANNABELL" and they all shouted out "HIP...HIP...HOORAY" at the end and a big cheer went up.

But Annabell had noticed something, she hadn't realised that ten of the eggs were different - it was only when ten little heads popped out of their shells that she noticed that they had different heads to all the others. They definitely were not Brachiosaurus. She had absolutely no idea what they were and neither did anyone else. But a Paleontologist was on hand - it was known to the government that there were ten different eggs which couldn't be identified, they wouldn't know what animals they were until they were born.

The Paleontologist examined the creatures and after consulting his reference book he declared that the creatures were in fact a Pterosaur from the same time as Pete. It was an ancestor of Bambalata's kind. Pterosaurs are not considered to be dinosaurs, but it didn't really matter.

Annabell was shocked but extremely pleased at the same time. The Pterosaur like the Brachiosaurus were harmless creatures. After some discussions with the United Nations delegates it was decided that they would be allowed to live on Earth but there was one problem. Pterosaurs can fly and they didn't want them to fly out of Dinosaur park. Annabell was consulted about this and it was agreed that when the creatures were able to understand Annabell she would tell them the rules about not flying out of the designated area which was considerable.

What a memorable day this had been, never to be forgotten! It was the greatest event the Earth had ever witnessed. The rebirth of the biggest dinosaurs that ever lived on Earth. But the day wasn't finished yet! The President asked Annabell to accompany him. They had a very special surprise that they had been scheming together with the permission of Mr and Mrs Jacobs. This was going to be something very special for the world to see.

Annabell and the President were gone for about fifteen minutes. Everybody knew that something was going to happen but what they saw was absolutely incredible.

The President of the United States of America lead out a nearly fully grown Brachiosaurus with Annabell sitting on its back! People stood there in awe of this unbelievable spectacle. The news media flashed their cameras. This picture would appear in every newspaper throughout the world

The years passed. *"ANNABELL'S DINOSUUR WORLD"* was a massive success, the baby dinosaurs flourished and were starting to have babies themselves. It was decided that other countries could build their own Dinosaur worlds to accommodate the new generation of animals that were being born. There were lots of new baby dinosaurs born every year. *"ANNABELL'S DINOSAUR WORLD"* was getting over crowded.

The first country to have the new baby dinosaurs was England. The Prime Minister of England and the President of The United States of America had always been close friends. Other countries would soon follow and have their own Dinosaur worlds. But it was decided that every one of them would have to include Annabell's name. So it became

"ANNABELL'S DINOSAUR WORLD OF ENGLAND" and whoever followed carried her name.

*

The adventures for Annabell were only just beginning.

The years passed. Annabell was now twenty-one years old.

It's the year 2222AD. The Devil's date!

Part two of Annabell's story will be told in the novel:

ANNABELL'S SEARCH FOR THE HOLISM

Children's books Kirkshaw Forest Stories Books. 1-2-3-4-5

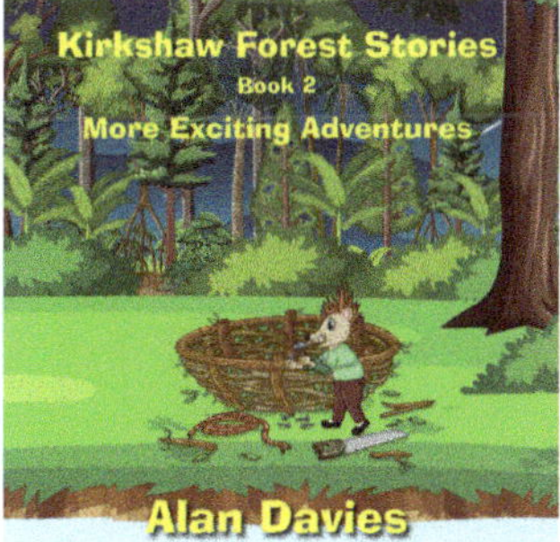

Children's book The Tablecloth Family Book 1	Young Adult & Adult book Captain Wirgoil's Challenge	Annabell's Search For The Holism – A Fantasy Novel